Ex Libris

Shelagh A. Murdock

Peacock in Flight

By the same author

_____

THE EMERALD PEACOCK

Peacock in Flight

1867-1868

by

Katharine Gordon

HODDER AND STOUGHTON
LONDON SYDNEY AUCKLAND TORONTO

British Library Cataloguing in Publication Data
Gordon, Katharine
    Peacock in Flight.
    I. Title
    823' .9'1F   PR6057.06/

    ISBN 0 340 23006 1

Chapter 1

The rising wind woke Bianca in the night from an uneasy sleep.

The old palace of Madore, the Madoremahal, was built to withstand all weathers. It was built exactly like all the palaces of the Hill rajas – replicas of their homes in their mountain States. None of the Hill rajas would have felt comfortable, or at home in any other type of dwelling place. The first Ruler of Lambagh, the great-uncle of the present Ruler was no exception. The Madoremahal was a copy of the old palace in Lambagh State, but greatly enlarged. It was almost empty now, more than half of it closed and unfurnished.

Now, in the night, hearing the wind rising outside, hearing the trees clashing their branches, and the shutters and doors creaking, Bianca was in a moment transported back to Lambagh, and waited to hear the lake begin to rise into miniature waves beneath her window; but all she heard was the dust and gravel blowing and the footsteps of the night watchman, old Lapsing, as he thumped past, closing windows and calling, as he always did, ' Sleep – sleep safely – all is well with the house.'

But Bianca could not sleep. She lay listening to the wind, and thinking of Lambagh. The wind had a voice, it spoke of the past and called to her – and it spoke of the future, and then, suddenly the wind seemed to say, ' Fifteen – it is time! She is fifteen. Remember your promise – '

She closed her eyes, and saw, clearly etched on her eyelids, a man's face, his grey eyes looking into her eyes as if he would see her heart there – she opened her eyes quickly, and lay with no thought of sleeping any more, only the memory of a promise – while the wind sighed and spoke to her about Lambagh.

Sara, her step-daughter, woke to the sound of the wind too, and lay listening to it with pleasure. To her, the Madoremahal seemed to have become a great carriage, a creaking, moving carriage, drawn by the wind, a carriage that would carry them all safely over the roads and the mountain passes to Lambagh. She smiled, and turned on her side, and slept again, while the wind rustled among the trees and rose higher, until the sky itself seemed to be blowing away.

In the morning the wind had dropped a little – the garden looked dusty, and some of the trees had lost branches, and the rooms were full of dust. Old Goki, who had been a woman servant in the family of the Lambagh Rulers since before Bianca was born, drove the house servants into activity as if she was a wind herself, so that the part of the Madoremahal that was in use should be clean and shining before Bianca came out of her room.

Having lain sleepless most of the night, Bianca was late coming out, and her part of the palace was spotless, as if there had been no wind in the night. But her night thoughts were still with her, like leaves blown into the corners of her mind.

Sara was already seated at the breakfast table, waiting for her, the sunlight reflecting back on her smiling face from the white cloth and the polished silver. Sara's eyes, lifted to her step-mother, were full of light, liquid, beautiful – she looked so happy, and so content. My blessed little Sara, thought Bianca, looking at her – at least you are happy, and whatever else happens you will always have the good things of life, always be comfortable and rich, but what will they do to your tender heart, up there in the mountains? What kind of a man will they find for you – will your heart be broken as mine was broken? God forbid. She looked at Sara's gentle, serene face, and as she looked, the girl said, ' Mother – the wind came in the night – the spring wind! Shall we go to Lambagh soon – Goki says we will be going soon – is it true? '

6

'Do you want to go so much? Don't you like your life here, Sara; have you been unhappy?'

'Oh, *Mother*! You know I have been happy. I love this place. But Lambagh is our home – and I am to be fifteen soon and Goki says – she has always said –'

'Goki talks too much. You are not fifteen yet. There are two months before your birthday. But, no doubt, this year we go. Now, eat, Sara and put some flesh on your bones. I do not understand how you are so thin.'

Sara, reaching for another chapatti, a flat thin griddle cake, shook her head.

'It is not because I do not eat, Mother. I have had curds and honey and four chapattis – this is my fifth – and two cups of coffee –'

'Heavens, child, spare me. I do not know where it all goes, but not on to your bones, anyway –' She stopped speaking, a sudden unwelcome memory of Sara's own mother stopping her in mid-speech. Kurmilla! The voluptuous body, the heavy lips and long slanted eyes, black as ripe plums. She searched Sara's face – certainly there was nothing of Kurmilla in Sara's build. She was as slim and supple as a boy. Only the high cheekbones and the tilted eyes, and the curved wide mouth showed her blood. Otherwise, with her clear grey eyes and slim frame, Sara looked like her young step-mother, who loved her as she had done from the moment she first saw her, as if she was her own child. There was so little difference in their ages, but Sara was the child of Bianca's heart.

Sara, her eyes dreaming, looked out at the green garden and thought of the snow-covered peaks round the blue lake of Lambagh, and of nothing else – until, suddenly reminded, she said, 'Kassim – he will come this evening?'

Bianca nodded.

'Yes, for supper, he said. Why? Is it so important?' Her voice was sharper than she meant it to be and Sara looked at her in surprise.

'No, but I hoped he would come early. I wished to show him

7

how well I am schooling Zuleika. She is so easy to ride now, her movements are like – '

' She is still half wild, Sara, please be careful. Kassim may come early, I know he has a great deal to say to me – '

A very great deal. No doubt he too would remind her of how the ten years had passed and of her promise – well, she would not leave before Sara's fifteenth birthday. She was surely entitled at least to these two months. But there was a voice deep within her, that said, ' You are entitled to nothing. She is not your child. You killed her mother and left her father of your own will – and you made a promise that you would return before her fifteenth birthday.'

She knew that Kassim would say exactly those words to her when he came – except that he would not speak of the killing of Kurmilla. No one ever mentioned that to her. She pushed back her chair suddenly, and walked out and down the steps to where the roses were blooming, hoping to find tranquillity among their scented perfection. But the sweet heavy smell of the Persian roses reminded her of the attar of roses that was used so profusely at weddings – and then, as she turned away, the wind began to rise again, but gently, and the roses, nodding crimson heads, seemed to be reminding her too – to be saying, ' Yes, you must take her back.'

With a sigh, Bianca returned to the house, where at least she could make herself busy, and shut out the wind, and the voices and memories that it brought to her.

But Sara walked in the garden, in the rising wind, with pleasure, and spent the morning in the stables, watching the horses being groomed, except for Zuleika – her own mare, a gift from Kassim. No one was allowed to groom her but Sara herself. When Zuleika's coat was shining like satin, and her flowing mane was combed until it looked like silk, Sara gave her a kiss in the middle of her soft nose and went back to the Madoremahal.

In the afternoon the wind gathered strength, and the rose petals were blown into heaps and then scattered again, and dust

8

dimmed the green grass.

'It is the spring wind – the wind that brings the hot weather,' thought Sara, and began to check over, in her mind, each town and village they would pass through on their way to the mountains.

The wind blew strongly, and the trees bent, and the bamboos that grew in clumps near the gate rustled and whispered. The bearers closed the shutters against the dusty wind, and the Madoremahal creaked and rattled as the wind talked.

Chapter 2

The wind that blew the rose petals about in the garden of the Madoremahal was the same wind that gusted over the dusty plain outside the walls of the Madoremahal and tugged at the coat of a man leading a limping horse over a rough track about four miles from the palace.

The wind flurried and blew dust into his eyes, making them sting and water. It made his mare throw up her head, tugging at her reins as she stumbled. Finally, the man stopped, with a curse, and looking round him chose a rock and sat with his back to the wind so that he and his mare, Bedami, were both sheltered.

Alan Reid was lost.

He had set out earlier that afternoon, thinking to ride along the river bank – but somewhere he had taken a wrong turn, and had been wandering for hours, until his mare had picked up a stone in a hoof, and he had had to dismount and lead her, limping himself in boots that were not intended for walking.

Now the swift Indian dusk was beginning to fall. He could see no landmarks, nothing that he could recognise. The plain stretched out on all sides of him, flat, dull, featureless. All the rocks looked alike, all the thorn bushes were identical. There did not appear to be a path to follow.

The mare, standing beside him, blew through her nostrils and whickered softly, and he put a gentle hand up to her neck.

' No good, old lady, we shall have to spend the night here,

and a damned uncomfortable night it is going to be – '

It was then that the goats came, skipping and running, brisk little black and white goats, all hurrying in one direction, obviously knowing their way. Alan stood up at once and pulled Bedami after him. Where there were goats, there was bound to be a goat-herd. Full of hope, he made the best speed he could, and sure enough, there was the goat-herd strolling through the dusk, tall and slim and young, and handsome enough to be the God Krishna himself, a flute in his hand.

' Thank God. Friend, can you tell me where Madore cantonments are? As you see, my mare is lame, and we have been lost for some hours.' Alan spoke in the fluent Urdu he had learned during his first two years in the army in India.

The goat-herd stopped and smiled at him.

' The Sahib is indeed lost. The cantonments lie some ten miles behind you, in that direction.' He ran a gentle hand down over the mare's swelling fetlock, lifted and examined the hoof, and stood up, shaking his head.

' Your mare can go very little distance, Sahib. Will it please you to come with me to the Madoremahal – my Mistress, the Begum of Lambagh will, I know, be glad to help you, and we can get that stone out.'

Alan would have gone anywhere to get shelter for himself and Bedami, and get his boots off.

' Lead on, friend.' The goats were now far ahead, almost out of sight. The goat-herd took Bedami's reins and began to walk slowly, with Alan, freed of Bedami, walking more easily behind him. Presently the goat-herd took up his flute and began to play, a gentle wavering little tune.

' Procession with music,' thought Alan and stumbled on.

After they had been walking for about twenty minutes, the goat-herd stopped playing, and stood listening. Above the wind Alan thought he could hear bells. The goat-herd took him by the arm and said, ' Come, Sahib – we go behind those rocks with your horse. Can you keep her quiet? '

Alan nodded and they went quickly behind a rampart of

rocks, where Alan put his hand firmly on Bedami's nose.

The bells grew louder and there was a soft padding sound, and a string of camels went by, each camel wearing a bell on its neck. There were about eight or nine men with the camels – tall fierce-looking men, with curved swords at their waists, their faces muffled with the ends of their turbans. They were sinister figures, moving past so silently, only the sound of bells marked their progress as they vanished into the dusk. After a few minutes the goat-herd moved forward and led the way out of the rocks and they set off again. Alan asked no questions – probably the camel drivers were known dacoits.

They turned a corner in the path that Alan could not see, round a great pile of rocks, and found the goats gathered in a close group in front of a high wooden gate set in a red plastered wall. The goat-herd rapped on the gates, and some unseen man opened them. The goats hurried through, the goat-herd pulled Bedami in and Alan followed him, and the gates were shut behind them.

The drive seemed to be long. Alan could smell the evening smell of freshly watered earth and flowers, and there were tall trees on each side of the drive, so that from the last of the twilight on the open plain, as the gate creaked shut behind him, Alan seemed to have entered darkness, as if the walls of the place he was in surrounded the night. It was an eerie feeling – Alan hurried after the goat-herd, and the goats, who knew their way and were not worried by the darkness, pattered ahead, and were suddenly gone.

Alan came out into a clear space, where light still lingered in the evening sky. A voice, husky and sweet called out something he did not understand, and he collided with someone with such force that he had to put out his hands to steady the person he had bumped into, or whoever it was would have fallen over. It was a girl, he found, and for a moment she stood still between his hands and it was as if he held a bird, so light and fragile seemed the body he held. He could not see her face – he had an impression for a minute, of enormous eyes, before, with an adroit twist, she freed herself and his hands were empty.

A voice spoke from behind her.

'Sara, what are you doing? Who is it?' It was an English voice, deep toned and clear. Alan answered at once.

'I beg your pardon for this intrusion, madam – I am Major Alan Reid from the 19/24th Lancers in Madore cantonments. I lost my way while out riding and my horse went lame – your goat-herd very kindly brought me to you –'

'Major Reid, you are most welcome. Please come in. Sara, tell Wazir to bring lamps. Can you see where you are, Major Reid? We have been sitting here in the evening light, so our eyes are used to it – but I know how dark our drive can be.'

Alan's eyes were growing used to the dim green dusk of the garden. There were steps in front of him, and the woman who was speaking to him was standing at the top of the steps. He climbed up to her and, bowing, said, 'Alan Reid, at your service, ma'am,' and received a deep curtsey in reply.

It was still too dark to see his hostess, but he could hear the girl's voice calling inside the house and then the woman's deep voice said, 'There is no question of you riding back – you can bathe, and have some supper and I will send you back in the landau. Ah, Wazir, take the Sahib to the Yuvraj's room and tell Goki to get some clean clothes.' His protests, only half-hearted in any case, were overruled. Alan followed the servant down a long passage and was shown into a large room where an oil lamp shone on Persian carpets and beautiful furniture, and an old woman stood salaaming in the middle of the room.

The old woman as she salaamed said, 'Greetings, Sahib. Your bath is ready – the room is through this door,' and showed no signs of leaving the room. Alan, sitting down to pull off his boots saw that she was laying out clean underwear, white jodhpurs and a silk shirt, on the bed. As he struggled with his boots, she came over and with great skill, and astonishing strength, pulled them off.

'Go, Sahib. When you have bathed I will rub your aches away.'

Alan hobbled, under her considering eye, into the bathroom, and found a large round marble tub let into the floor, and a big earthenware jar full of steaming water with a dipper beside it. He splashed and poured and felt the water, hot and soothing, reviving him.

When he returned to the bedroom, prudently draped in a towel, the old woman was waiting for him, with a bottle of Cognac and a silver goblet – and a determined face.

'Lie on the bed, Sahib. Ah, such modesty! I am old enough to be the grandmother of your mother, and I have no fear of what I might see. Lie, and let my hands take away your stiffness.' Protests were obviously hopeless. Towelless and resigned Alan lay down, and felt her hands, hard and strong, begin to knead and slap and pound on his back and hips. She gave him a goblet of brandy and in between her thumps and strokings he drank.

Presently, under her steady kneading up and down his spine and from neck to ankles he found he was almost falling asleep. He forced himself awake and saw that the window of the room opened on to a courtyard, where a large fire was burning. As he watched, a woman came out to throw more wood on the fire. He saw her face, illuminated by the leaping flames, and wondered if every woman in the house was a raving beauty. This girl was a servant; she wore a full long skirt and a *choli*, a short, tight-fitting bodice. Her head cloth had slipped back and he could see her luxuriant long hair, plaited and hanging almost to her waist. She was laughing, with a splendid flash of white teeth in a red curved mouth, and as the flames leapt higher he saw the man she was talking to – a tall man, his head bound in a black turban. Alan was suddenly broad awake: surely that was one of the camel drivers he had hidden from on the road? – as he looked, the man put a hand to his loose robes and pulling something out, gave it to the girl. Alan could see the expression of pleasure on her face, and then the flash of gold as she raised her hands to her ears – first one and then the other – and he saw that she was putting on golden earrings. Well, she was a pretty wench, perhaps it was for services rendered.

The fire died down and he could not see. Afterwards he was to regret with all his heart that he had not drawn the old woman's attention to what he had seen. When the fire next burned brightly, blown into life by the wandering wind, the courtyard was empty.

Chapter 3

'Well, Sahib, I think you feel better. Nay, do not worry, here is your towel. Drink your brandy and then I leave you to dress.'

Goki poured him out another generous tot and as he drank it, settled herself down to massage his legs and showed herself very willing to answer his discreet questions.

'My mistress? The Begum Bianca. She is the wife of the Ruler of Thinpahari. Her daughter is the Begum of Thinpahari.'

'Great heavens, but I have a friend, my very good friend, Major Kassim Khan Behadur – the Yuvraj of Thinpahari – '

'So, you know Kassim Khan Behadur, the heir? How does it come about that you know him?'

'He is of my regiment.'

'Oho, is that how the Sahib comes to speak our tongue so well?' Under her seasoned eyes, Alan blushed.

'No, I learned – I had many lessons in Lucknow when I was there for two years.'

'Aha, yes. That is the best way to learn. A pretty little whore in your *bibighar,* and you learn more than any *munshi* could ever teach you. Sahib – indeed you are very modest. Is shame attached to manhood in your country? All the British officers – if they are sensible – learn our language on the pillow. Ah me – ' She sighed a wicked sigh.

'How I wish I was sixty years younger – in my twenties I would have enjoyed teaching you many things. A fine man, Sahib, with a fine body. Nothing better could happen to a woman. I would have taken great pleasure in teaching you.'

'Indeed, you do me honour, Lady of great experience. I feel sure you could have taught me many things – I regret that we have met at the wrong time. I was born too late, alas.'

'Oh, and a tongue of honey as well – Now, Sahib, let us have no more of the towel and the blushes. I will help you dress, and you will be ready quickly – the Begum Sahiba waits –'

Inhibitions removed by Cognac and her laughter, he allowed her to help him dress as he would have accepted the ministrations of his bearer. As she smoothed the silk shirt over his shoulders he asked to whom the clothes belonged.

'But who do you think? Kassim Khan Behadur, who else? You must be of a size – let us see if you can wear his shoes, for I do not think you will be able to put your boots on. There – a perfect fit. Now, Sahib, if you will follow me –'

As he followed her down the long passage, he wondered why Kassim, who had become his closest friend in the Regiment, had never mentioned that he had relatives in Madore – and then stopped wondering about anything as he went into the room where his hostess and her daughter were waiting for him.

It was a large room, furnished in rich native style, with many cushioned divans and magnificent carpets and heavy silk hangings. It was a beautiful room, a fit setting for the two women who waited for him.

His hostess was one of the most beautiful young women he had ever seen. She sank, with polished grace, into a deep curtsey – as he rose from his bow, he looked down into wide thickly lashed blue eyes, that did not smile as her mouth smiled. Her eyes were beautiful, but quite inscrutable. Her hair, coiled high on her head was streaked liberally with white, and yet her face was the cameo face of a young woman. He found himself staring, bowed again, thanking her for her kindness, and looked at the other occupant of the room.

But this was not a grown woman. She was a very young girl. She was beautiful too. She had slanted silver grey eyes above high cheekbones, and a curved full-lipped red mouth. The long length of her straight black hair on the loose cream brocade robe she wore, shone in the lamplight like black water under the moon. Her skin was the colour of very creamy coffee. She was as exotic as the room, as the scent of jasmine and *champak* blossom that drifted in from the garden. She was very small, and the brocade robe hung as flat as a boy's would have done. She was sitting, curled like a cat on the cushions of a low divan, a silver lamp beside her. He bowed to her, and she rose easily, and joined her hands palm to palm, bending her head over them in the graceful salutation of India. Alan thought she was fascinating, a lovely child – and she raised her eyes and looked at him. He wondered how old she was, and her mother's voice behind him, suggesting that he might care for some Cognac before they ate, brought him back in time before his stare became embarrassing.

There was a silver goblet in his hand, his hostess seated herself gracefully among her full skirts, the girl curled down among the cushions, and Alan, answering kind questions about his comfort was afraid to drink – he felt already as if he was a little drunk, and dizzy with tiredness and an enchanted strangeness. The girl did not speak. She sat by the open window, and her stillness was the immobility of someone who waits and listens.

Servants had laid a table, and there was the savoury smell of food. Alan drank slowly, watching the Begum Bianca drink from her silver goblet and wondered if she had ever made an ungraceful movement in her life. When, at last, he had finished his Cognac, she offered him wine, saying, ' My nephew is late – but we will not wait too long for him. You must be so hungry.' As she spoke, her daughter raised her head.

' He comes,' she said softly, and into the room came the sound of a horse being ridden hard.

' Kassim rides always as if the devil pursued him,' said the Begum Bianca, and got up, her skirts swaying from her slim waist like the petals of a flower.

The hoofbeats came up the drive and stopped and a deep voice called a greeting, and the girl still sat, her eyes on the door. Then booted feet ran up the steps, and Kassim Khan

18

Behadur, heir to the throne of Thinpahari and Major in Alan's regiment, came into the room.

He looked at the girl, and she smiled at him, and then he turned to her mother.

' Forgive me, Bianca – I am very late. A friend of mine went riding today and has not returned and I have been searching for him – '

Something made him turn his head, and for a moment he stopped speaking and stared at Alan as if he had never seen him before. Then he said slowly, ' Great Azrael – what are you doing here? ' His voice sounded far from friendly.

' Kassim! What a greeting! This is Major Reid, he too has been lost and Rama found him and brought him here – '

' I know Major Reid very well – I have just spent nearly four hours looking for him. Alan, you fool, where have you been? I was about to send out a search party. I am delighted to find you in such good hands – of course, you have never met my aunt, the Begum of Lambagh – and her daughter the Begum Sahiba of Thinpahari – until now.' He paused and then turned to the girl.

' Sarajan – how are you? Did you ride? '

' I rode. I waited to show you how well I rode, but you did not come.'

' No – you can blame Major Reid for that. I could not leave my friend lost and wandering – though I might have known the devil looks after his own. Alan – you look exhausted – how did you manage to lose yourself? '

Feeling a fool under Kassim's laughing eyes, Alan said stiffly, ' I do not know – I took the road that I thought led to the banks of the Kanti and found myself in the middle of nowhere – I was so grateful to meet the Begum's goat-herd – but I apologise for intruding into your family like this – '

' My dear Major Reid, you are very welcome. It is easy to get lost in the Rakh, and I am delighted that Rama found you. Now, come and eat – Kassim, no doubt after all your exertions on Major Reid's behalf, you are also hungry.'

19

Seated in comfort at the candlelit table, eating well-cooked food and drinking good wine, the dream-like feeling that Alan had felt earlier, grew stronger. He felt he was under some enchantment and that at the clap of hands the whole scene would vanish and he would find himself sitting alone in the desert with his mare drooping beside him. He spoke very little, and spent his time watching the others and listening. The girl also was very quiet. The Begum Bianca and Kassim had plenty to say to each other. There appeared to be a disagreement between them, which showed itself in a constant sparring of words. Alan saw the girl looking from one to the other as a frown deepened on Kassim's face and a sharp note rang every now and then in the Begum Bianca's husky, beautiful voice.

Presently, between one sentence and another, the subject seemed to have changed – Alan heard Kassim say sharply, ' But it is after all ten years, Bianca – and whether you believe me or not, I tell you we should go. I *must* go – I gave my word. Did you not give yours? '

' It is not ten years for another two months – '

' By that time, anything could have happened.'

' Such as? '

' Bianca, you are being foolish. Do I have to tell you? '

' In truth, yes, because you are speaking in riddles, Kassim. There is no hurry that I know of. In two months the weather will be better – those mountain passes at this time of year will still be under snow. Besides, there is so much to do before we leave.'

' What is there to do? '

' Oh, Kassim! There are preparations for the journey. The Madoremahal must be closed and dust covers put over all the furniture; the horses must be readied, mules and mule drivers engaged – perhaps palanquin coolies should come down from Lambagh – '

Kassim pushed back his chair, and picking up his goblet, drained it in one long swallow.

' My dear aunt, you invent obstacles. However, I will say no more, but I advise you to think well before you delay. You know what we all fear.' He turned to Alan. ' This is very boring for you, Alan. We are discussing my leave. I am going up to Lambagh to see my uncle, and as the two Begums have to go as well, I thought it would be good if they came with me as their escort. What do you think? '

' Apart from the fact that you and I were, I thought, going on a shooting trek together for our joint leave, I envy you going up into the mountains – and if the ladies go with you, then I envy you your company.'

' My dear Alan – our shooting trip – how rude of me to forget. I have had a great deal to think about today – we must discuss our trip later. As for envying me my company – it will be like travelling with the whole regiment, and all their wives and camp followers – and I remember well how much you enjoyed our transfer from Lucknow! '

' Really, Kassim, you do me great honour, and Sara too, comparing us to camp followers. Come, Major Reid, let us all take our wine and sit more comfortably.' She got up and led the way back to the drawing-room, where once more Sara dropped bonelessly into the cushions by the window and Kassim said firmly, ' In these breeches I cannot collapse on to cushions, Sara, so I shall bring a chair over and sit beside you – tell me about Zuleika.'

They talked together, Bianca joining in, about Sara's horse and her riding – while Alan, muzzy with wine and exhaustion, fell deeper into enchantment and sat watching Sara's face and her long-fingered hands playing with a white rose she had picked up from a bowl beside her. The more he looked at her, the more she enthralled him. Everything about her seemed perfect. He could not turn his eyes away and lost all sense of what the others were talking about. All he could see were Sara's sparkling tilted eyes, and her delicate brown hand holding and turning the white rose.

Presently Kassim came over to him.

' Alan, you are falling asleep. Bianca, I think we should take our leave. We have a long ride back. Alan, is your mare able for it?'

'But there is no question of you riding back. Please do not be ridiculous, Kassim. I will send Fagir Ali over tomorrow with the horses, I have already ordered the brougham. Dost Mohammed will bring it round shortly. Give Major Reid another drink and stop being so impatient.'

'I think Major Reid has had enough wine – he is three parts asleep already.'

Alan, rousing himself, refuted this, and accepted a glass of wine he did not really want. Kassim poured a stiff Cognac for himself, and looking over at Sara said, 'You are very quiet tonight – what are you dreaming about?'

The girl turned at once to smile at him.

'I am thinking of the journey, and of the valley.' A flash of pleasure lit Kassim's eyes, and he smiled at her. 'Well, at least one of us is ready to leave for Lambagh with pleasure. I take it you would leap on to Zuleika's back and leave at once.'

'I will help my mother,' said Sara sedately. 'And I will be ready to leave when she is.'

Bianca and Kassim looked at each other, and Bianca looked down at her hands after a moment, under his straight gaze. He spoke very low, so that only she could hear him.

'You have great influence over her, Bianca – see that you do not use it to cause her harm.' She looked up to reply, her eyes full of anger, but just in time there was the crunch of gravel on the drive outside, and the sound of jingling harness. The brougham had been brought round.

Chapter 4

The two men bowed themselves out, Alan asking permission to call on them shortly, and Bianca telling him to please come whenever he wished. The old bearer led them out to the carriage, and as they settled themselves back in the cushioned seats, the two horses were released, the Syce jumped up beside the driver and the wheels and the clop of horses' hooves drowned the farewells from the top of the steps, and they were off.

The two men were silent, Kassim sitting looking out at the darkness, Alan lost in his own thoughts. The dream-like quality of the evening was still with him – how strange that those two fascinating women should be the relatives of the man he knew best in the regiment, and whom he had thought of as his close friend.

Kassim spoke first.

' You enjoyed your evening? '

' Very much.' Alan spoke slowly, trying to find words to describe how he had felt when he arrived at the Madoremahal.

' It was like a dream – what a beautiful place, and what beautiful women – I have never seen such beauty. Your cousin is breathtaking and your aunt also. Why did you never mention them before, Kassim? And you never brought them to any of the garden parties or the balls.' Kassim's laugh was dry.

' Now, Alan – you know better than that! Can you imagine that they would be welcome at any of the parties – when I myself, the Yuvraj of Thinpahari, have heard myself decribed as " the half-caste officer "? In any case, since the Mutiny, Indian women have not been seen at European parties. You must know that! '

Alan nodded. ' Yes – of course. More tragedy and disaster followed that ghastly affair than one could have imagined. But your aunt is English, is she not? '

The quality of the silence between them after he had spoken was different. For the first time in all their friendship, Alan realised that he was talking to a man of another race, and a very proud man. When Kassim answered, his voice had changed.

' And that makes all the difference? As a matter of fact, my aunt, the wife of the Ruler of Thinpahari, is Irish. But she is of course only married to an Indian Prince. Her daughter is not in fact her own child – she is the daughter of the Ruler's first wife, who was a Southern woman whose antecedents were uncertain but it is suspected that her mother, the Rani of Natch, bore her to an Irish plate layer, though her husband the Raja was a good man, and gave her his name. But in spite of all this mixed blood, my aunt would certainly have no desire to mix with Madore cantonment society. She would find it very dull.'

In spite of Kassim's hard, cold voice, Alan could not restrain his curiosity.

' Kassim, why does the Begum not live in Lambagh with your uncle? '

' Alan, you have stumbled into my family and of course long to know their story. Listen, then. I will tell you as briefly as I can. Please – I do not have to ask you to be silent about what I tell you? ' Alan looked at him without speaking, and Kassim nodded. ' Very well. Listen.'

As he heard the story of Bianca's life, and of how she came to be living away from her husband, Alan felt he was hearing about somebody's nightmare, a ghastly series of events that could only be part of a horror filled dream. Kassim's voice peopled the darkness with shadowy figures and events. Alan heard of the beautiful young Bianca's escape from the disasters of the Mutiny, and her marriage to the Ruler of Thinpahari. He heard of their great happiness which ended in tragedy when Bianca rescued the five-year-old Sara from a burning house and so injured herself that she lost the baby she was carrying and could never have another child. He heard with horror of how the Ruler's first wife had kidnapped Bianca, drugged her, and assisted her cousin Hardyal to rape her. Kassim's voice was as sombre as the great empty dark plain that they were crossing. ' Bianca killed the woman – stabbed her to death in front of all the people of the valleys, on the day she made her dedication vows with Sher Khan, as the consort of the Ruler. Then she refused the honour of being the Rani of the three States. She could no longer bear the touch of a man – and my uncle sent her down here, hoping that living alone, in a place she loves, would cure her. He has lived alone for ten years – and that was the time limit. He made Bianca promise to return in ten years, with Sara. When Bianca resigned her place as Rani, Sher Khan, the Ruler, made Sara, his daughter, the Rani of the three States. But Bianca was greatly loved by the people – and they call her the Begum of Lambagh. It has been a terrible thing for my uncle, this gap in their lives – and it has also been very sad for me.'

Kassim spoke in a sombre voice that fitted the darkness in which they sat.

' You see, I could think of no way to tell him about the rape of Bianca. He was furious with me for not telling him, and said that he would never trust me again. I was young, and devoted to him, admired him more than any man I knew, and I was very proud. We parted in anger, and I left my country, and came down into India and joined the army. He made me promise to return in ten years, and this I am about to do. I love my uncle very much. We are close in age, he is only thirty-eight, and was my friend. I hope that time has healed the wound for him, as it has for me.'

' He was your father's brother ? '

' No – my father, dear Alan, was a man of your race. You knew that! Charles Edward Skene, Colonel in the 84th Light Cavalry. My mother is the Begum Mumtaz, Sher Khan's eldest sister. When my father died, I was fifteen. My mother brought me back to Lambagh then.'

' It must have been very hard for you, after being away all your life. Were you unhappy? '

' Strangely, no. I was at home at once. I missed my father very much, of course, but I did not miss England. It is not easy to be the child of a mixed marriage. My mother is a wonderful woman, and she worshipped my father, and therefore did not notice any slights that might have been put upon her. You are a very insular race, you English, in your own country. And your schoolboys have many ways of tormenting anything they find strange. I disliked particularly being called " Coffee Khan ".'

Alan thought of Kassim's splendid looks, his clear grey eyes, his fierce pride, and imagined that he might well have objected to being called ' Coffee Khan '.

Beside him, Kassim stirred, and sighed. ' Well – it is over now. I am home. And it is time for Bianca to take Sara home. She must not delay.'

As he was speaking, the carriage stopped, and Kassim leaned forward, his hand feeling, as Alan's was, for his pistol. But the driver turned and said, ' All is well, Kassim Khan – but I would speak to you, and this is a good place. Is it possible I speak to you alone? '

Alan at once said, ' I will go and wait beside the road – I feel like stretching my legs, and I have a great deal to think about.'

Kassim put his arm round his shoulders.

' No, Alan – let there be no question of you going anywhere. It is good that you should hear what Dost Mohammed has to say. Come, Dost Mohammed, speak freely. The Sahib is as my brother – you have news? '

Dost Mohammed climbed up and sat facing them in the carriage. ' Yea. Bad news. Hardyal is released by the British and has come up from the south. He speaks much of his rights – '

' Rights? '

' Lord, he claims that as Kurmilla's cousin, and as he was married to Khanzada your aunt who died in the bad year of

'57, through these relationships, he claims the right to the throne of Lambagh. Also, he speaks of the young Begum – ' Alan was conscious of the sudden fury that made Kassim's voice shake when he spoke to Dost Mohammed.

' Oh? And what, pray, does he say of the young Begum? '

' He speaks of marriage, Lord – '

' The dog – the son of a noseless mother! Does he so? His flesh will be eaten by the wolves of the three States when I have finished with him.'

' There is more, heaven born.'

' Speak.'

Alan sat silent and listened, his mind whirling at the stories Dost Mohammed told. Hardyal he had heard of before – he had been a prisoner of the British for ten years, he was a murderer and a known agitator, and now it appeared he was a close relative of Kassim, and had been released from prison. According to Dost Mohammed he was involved in an arms deal, smuggling guns up from a port in south India, and selling them to the tribes on the North-West Frontier, where there was always trouble. As Kassim's quick questions brought out the most astonishing and terrible stories of unrest in the city of Madore and the surrounding district, Alan listened with growing alarm. The darkness and the lowered voices, and the silence all around them added horror to the slowly unfolding story. At the end, when Dost Mohammed stopped speaking, Kassim sat quiet, and Alan, with questions fighting each other in his brain, did not say anything, but watched the lamplight flickering on the road, and then realised uneasily that Dost Mohammed was watching not the lamplight, but the shadows, and that his watchfulness was as tense as that of a crouching leopard. He too began to stare into the darkness, and to wish that they had stopped elsewhere to talk. This place was too easily overlooked.

Kassim's laugh made him jerk nervously, and he turned, frowning.

' Alan, do not worry. Dost Mohammed always sits like a leopard in a branch. This place is safe enough, and safer than trying to talk between four walls. Well, one thing must be obvious to you now – the reason why I am so anxious for Bianca and Sarajan to leave for Lambagh. And it is not safe for them to travel alone. Hardyal is as dangerous as a mad dog – and he is almost here. You heard Dost Mohammed saying he was in Sultankote three days ago, and has already caused trouble there, stirring up inter-communal riots to cover his own doings!' He sat thinking again, and then began to give Dost Mohammed explicit instructions about men who were to go from the lines of the 17/24th Lancers to guard the Madoremahal. Alan broke in : 'Kassim, these are all men of our companies – yours and mine – will they get leave in time?'

'They have all been granted leave already. I had warning earlier and have been preparing as well as I could. But I forgot my own leave – Alan, you will help me here – my leave is not due for another week, and I must go tomorrow. Can you take a leave chit to the adjutant for me – what is it, do you not wish to become involved in my family matters? I do not blame you.'

Alan looked at him. 'Kassim, this is the second time you have come within an ace of offending me. Our shooting leave. Remember? Mine starts tomorrow. We have been discussing this for weeks – everyone has heard us, which is good. Tomorrow morning, I shall take my leave certificate, and yours, and Jeavons will still be thick-headed from the night before and will sign anything. Then we are both free for three months.'

Kassim's raised eyebrows could not be seen in the dark, but his feelings sounded in his voice when he said slowly, 'Alan, you are a king among men. Our shooting trip! Of course. We will be a large party on this shooting trip, and I expect we will get very little shooting – unless it is big game. Now all I have to do is to persuade Bianca to move fast. How soon after tomorrow's early parade can you get yourself and your kit to the Madoremahal?'

'My mare Bedami is lame. I shall need one of your horses – which one? My kit is already packed and a pack mule will take it. I can be at the Madoremahal by nine tomorrow morning.'

' Alan, as I said, you are a king. Take Zenobia – you have a predilection for mares. My kit – what part of it you are not wearing – is already in the Madoremahal. Bring your man Kullunder Khan with you, he is a good man and comes from the hills. Now we go on. Dost Mohammed, you know what to do – and may Allah assist us all.'

Back in his own quiet room, with the miniatures of his father and mother on the wall, his polo sticks in a corner, and his uniform put ready for the early parade, Alan wondered if he had been dreaming. The whole evening took on, in retrospect, an unreal quality; Alan felt like a man waking from a dream he could only half remember. But as he sat, looking round him, there was a light tap on the door, and Kassim came in, his face very grave.

' Alan, there is more need for haste than I thought. My servant Yusuf is dead.'

' *Dead?* How? '

' He was laying out my uniform for the morning – and there was a snake inside the pocket of my coat – if he had not put a clean kerchief in, I would have been the one to die. That snake could not have got into my pocket alone. It was a krait.'

Alan shuddered. A krait was a very small, very deadly snake. He looked at his own uniform, and back at Kassim, and his face was very pale. Alan had a horror of snakes. Kassim nodded. ' Yes, my friend. From now on, for God's sake be very careful. Kullunder is coming to you now – he will check the room. I am going back to Madore – and I will see you in the morning, if Allah wills.'

Kullunder Khan came in as Kassim left, and under Alan's eye went over the room, searching every corner and shaking out all his clothes, until they were both satisfied that there was nothing dangerous in the room. Then Kullunder Khan stretched out on the floor in front of the door, and Alan lay on his bed, with no thought of sleep, until the false dawn began to lighten the sky briefly, and it was time for him to get up and dress.

Chapter 5

It all went so easily.

Captain Jeavons, the adjutant, had a very thick head after a night's dissipation, and groaning, signed the leave application without any comment. He had heard the shooting trek discussed in detail over the mess table for weeks, and did not notice that Kassim's leave had been put forward by a week. Alan returned to his quarters, collected Kullunder Khan and the fidgeting mare Zenobia, and set off for the Madoremahal, arriving to find the gate guarded by two of his own men, Osman Khan and Walli Mohammed, who grinned companionably at him, and swung the great gates open. He noted with interest that they were armed with their own issue Lee-Enfield rifles, and rode on down the drive to find himself in the middle of what appeared to be a breakfast party, with Kassim Khan and the Begum Bianca quarrelling furiously and Sara sitting quietly drinking coffee.

The Begum Bianca said good morning to him, a man ran up from the stables to take his horse and tell him that his mule and baggage had arrived. The old bearer, Wazir, came out on to the wide marble terrace with fresh coffee and hot chapattis, and Alan was part of the breakfast party.

Kassim was looking very angry, and he barely acknowledged Alan's arrival. He turned to Bianca as soon as he had said ' Good morning ' and continued a discussion which had obviously been going on for some time.

' I do not understand why you are being so foolish. I tell you,

Hardyal is on his way here – and he is coming for Sara. Can you go on sitting there, telling me that it is ridiculous to leave in such a hurry – Bianca, you should know how dangerous he is.'

A spasm twisted Bianca's face, making it almost ugly – an expression of such sorrow and desolation that Alan could not look at her, and Sara got up and went round to her mother and put her arms round her.

Bianca was very tired. Late in the night, when she was lying sleepless, old Goki had come into her room silently and asked permission to speak.

'The devil is loose, Bianca. The British have released him. They say – '

'Oh Goki – always "They say". *Who* says? Are you bringing me bazaar rumours again, and in the middle of the night?'

'No, Bianca *jenab* – I bring you no rumours. He is indeed free, and already Sultankote is in flames. He comes this way, and has stated that he will take Sara and marry her, and through her the Peacock chain and the Rulership of the three States.'

'That is ridiculous.' Bianca spoke calmly, above the tumult of horror that was trying to drown her judgment. 'No one inherits the throne of the three States while the Ruler still lives – and we would have heard if anything had happened to him. Also – have you forgotten that Kassim Khan is the heir?'

'No, I forget nothing, lady. But the servant of Kassim Khan Behadur lies dead – he put a kerchief into the pocket of Kassim's uniform coat and there was a krait in the pocket. If his man were not dead, the snake would have killed the Yuvraj, as it was intended to do. The Yuvraj is here – do you wish to see him?'

A snake in the pocket of Kassim's coat – Bianca shuddered. But she shook her head. 'No, let the Yuvraj sleep now. I will see him in the morning.'

'Have you forgotten your promise, Bianca?'

'What promise, presumptuous one?'

'Maybe I am presumptuous. But I have known you all your life, Bianca, and loved you, and I cannot allow you to be foolish.

You promised to take Sarajan back to her father in ten years. Ten years have almost passed, and in the face of great danger you are delaying. You are wrong – for Sara's sake we must go.'

' Goki, you are old, and need your sleep. You have delivered your warning, now go. We can make decisions in the morning, when our heads are clear.'

Goki looked at her mistress in silence, and had a sudden memory of this beautiful stern woman as she had been one day many years ago, standing in the full flower of her girlhood, saying, ' I know what I want – I want to stay in this country with Sher Khan as my Lord, for the rest of my life.' She looked at Bianca now, lying against her pillows, still young and beautiful, twenty-six years old, with only her white streaked hair to show what disasters had befallen her – stared down at her mistress with eyes that saw both the past and the present.

Bianca looked away from her, and said again, ' Goki, go. I need my sleep. We will speak in the morning.' Goki turned away and went without a word.

In the morning Lapsing, the old watchman, was found dead, a dagger in his back, and while Bianca was still assimilating all that this meant, Kassim Khan came out of his room, demanding that she left at once, with Sara – that very day.

She was terrified by the thought of the return to Lambagh. All these painful, lonely years, she had slowly fought her way back to sanity, so that she could sleep at night without waking up screaming, and could give her hand to a man without feeling the shuddering horror of one who touches a snake. Now she was faced with a journey that would end all her peace – and what were they going to do with Sara, beautiful tender-hearted Sara, who had been so happy with her? A voice in her heart told her that Sara would be even happier in the mountains and valleys of Lambagh – and with a sigh she forced her mind back from thoughts of the night before, and listened to what Kassim was saying, the anger in his voice barely controlled.

' You should know how dangerous he is – to both of you – '

She put Sara's loving, clinging arms aside, and said, ' Yes,

Kassim Khan, as you say, I should know.' Kassim stared at her, and then leant over her and took her hand.

'Bianca. Forgive me. I did not mean to hurt you. You know that. But I do not know why you delay like this.'

'Because I cannot help feeling that we are, for the moment, safer here, well guarded by your men, near to a British cantonment, than we would be fleeing to the hills, away from British jurisdiction, with Hardyal hot on our heels.'

'I was inside a British cantonment when my servant died, bitten by a snake that had been put in my coat pocket – and last night, old Lapsing was murdered.'

Bianca thought of faithful old Lapsing, and his nightly cry 'Sleep – sleep safely. All is well with the house.' There was no safety anywhere on the plains with Hardyal free. With a sudden collapse of all her arguments, she said wearily, 'Very well, Kassim. We leave. But we cannot leave today. I can be ready by tomorrow morning. Will that please you?'

'It would please me better if we went now.'

'Well, we cannot, Kassim, it is a ten-day journey. We need provisions. I have servants who will come with me, we must have the Madoremahal made secure.'

'Very *well*. But *when* do we leave?'

'Will dawn tomorrow please the Yuvraj?' Kassim ignored the sarcasm in her voice.

'No. But it is better than any more delay. So, we leave at dawn tomorrow. Now, Bianca, this is how we will go –'

A shadow fell across the white cloth – all four of them looked up, to see a girl standing beside them, a coffee pot in her hands. Far darker skinned than most of the Indians of the north, she was very beautiful in her full scarlet skirt and *choti*, the tight-fitting short bodice that outlined her full breasts, and her smile was brilliant as she held out the silver coffee pot on a tray, asking if the heaven-born wished for more coffee. But Bianca did not smile at her.

'What are you doing here, Lalla? Where is Wazir? Why are you not doing your own work? There is plenty of cleaning to be done. Put the coffee pot here, and send Wazir to me – '

Lalla put the coffee pot down and turned to leave with an insolent swirl of hips and skirt. Alan, seeing the curve of her neck, leading up to a delicate ear with a golden earring hanging in it, suddenly remembered the girl beside the fire in the courtyard, and the tall man in the dress of a camel driver, who had been with her.

Before he could speak, Kassim said, ' Who is she? '

' She is the daughter of one of the sweepers – an untouchable. Too pert and pretty for her own good. She has nothing to do here, near our table. I do not know what Wazir was thinking of, to let her bring the coffee – '

' What was I saying just as she came up? '

Alan answered him. ' You said something about leaving at dawn.'

' Had I mentioned our route? '

' No – Kassim, I saw that girl last night. She was talking to a camel driver, a very tall man, here in the courtyard, and he gave her gold – the earrings that I think she wears this morning.'

Bianca and Kassim both stared at him.

' Go on, Alan – '

' There is nothing more – the camel driver was a tall man, in a black turban – '

Kassim turned at once to Bianca.

' What was a camel driver doing here? '

' I do not know anything about it.' Bianca sounded worried and frightened.

' You say he was very tall, Alan? Bianca, I am afraid dawn tomorrow is too late. We leave today, as soon as possible.'

Bianca nodded. Wazir, the bearer, came out, and was questioned. ' Nay, Huzoor – I would not send that one with your coffee! She must have picked up the pot when I was not looking – I shall go and deal with her.'

' *No,* Wazir,' said Kassim suddenly. ' Bring her back here. I want to talk to her – '

But ten minutes later, Wazir came back to say that Lalla could

34

not be found, and Kassim turned to Bianca.

' Well? '

' Yes. You are right. Have I an hour? '

' Yes, but no more. We should not stay as long as that. I will send the men with our baggage by another route – that may confuse any pursuit.' He stopped speaking as Bianca raised her hand.

' Listen – Kassim, what is that noise? '

If a hive of bees had been upset, the angry buzzing would have been the same as the sound that carried on the breeze from the direction of the city, about three miles away. The buzzing was punctuated by two or three isolated shots – and then, as if their ears had become attuned to the noise they heard clearly the sounds of an angry mob.

' That is a riot, and a big one. Bianca, change into your habit, get Goki, and we go. We now have two dangers to face and one of them is a recall from leave – the regiment will certainly be sent in there. Sara – Alan, go with Sara to the stables and get the horses. Sara, you do *not* ride Zuleika, she is not properly broken. You ride Safed. Understood? I go to the gate to warn our men to stay out of sight or they will be collected if the regiment goes this way – Bianca, remember, change your clothes and come. We have very little time now.'

Bianca was already hurrying away, and Alan saw Goki coming out to meet her. Sara touched his arm. ' Do you come with me to the stables? '

He followed her and was suddenly mesmerised by her walk. This child walked with all the grace and seduction of a trained dancer, every movement she made was graceful, but there was something more, something that even in this moment of crisis set his pulses racing. All he could think of suddenly was the feel of her body between his hands when he had held her for a moment the night before. They arrived at the stables and Alan could hardly look away from her as she gave orders to the syces. Her voice, deep and husky, her profile, turned towards him as she watched the horses brought out, was so different from any

ideal of beauty he had ever had before that he could not under-
stand what made him stare at her face, possessed, enchanted.
With his whole mind and body in a turmoil, he heard her say
' Major Reid – ' and realised that she had been speaking to him.
  ' I beg your pardon – '
  ' I only asked you to look at Zuleika – is she not beautiful? '
The chestnut mare, standing deceptively still in front of them
was certainly beautiful. The syce held her easily, but Alan saw
that the horse was very jumpy – her ears twitched constantly,
pricking forward and then back as the noises from the city
increased, and a rattle of gunfire sounded clearly in the air and
set her dancing, almost pulling the syce off his feet. Sara went
forward at once.
  ' Now, my beautiful – sooo – she needs riding, that is all.
What a pity Kassim won't let me ride her on this trek. Safed
will be like sitting in a boat. Now, see how quiet she is with me? '
  Alan saw that indeed the mare was whickering with pleasure,
her soft nose buried in Sara's shoulder, as she rubbed the arching
neck.
  ' Oh, darling Zuleika – I *will* take you, and ride you on the
way. Suffi, get Safed out and saddle him for me, and Major
Reid's mare – look, Major Reid, how easy she is now – I can ride
her bareback.' She was up on the mare's back, with no saddle
and only a light snaffle and bridle – and the mare stood like a
rock, as quiet as she had been restive before. As Alan looked at
Sara's laughing face, there was another rattle of gunfire from the
city, and at the same time one of the syces pushed open a
creaking door. The combined noises were too much – Zuleika
went off like a rocket and Alan watched paralysed as he saw
her go through the stable gates and clear a thorn hedge like a
bird flying over, with Sara sitting firmly on her back. Then he
ran shouting for the first horse that was saddled and as he
mounted he saw Rama the goat-herd coming into the stable
yard and yelled at him to tell the Yuvraj what had happened.
  ' Tell him we are in the Rakh – I have gone after the Begum.
Tell him she was going towards the sun – ' There was no time

36

for more – he set his big horse at the high thorn hedge, took it, and was over and out in the open country, following the dust cloud that marked Sara's progress.

He came up with her as she entered a small stand of trees, and by that time to his amazed admiration she had Zuleika under control. He could hear water, and realised that they were near the Kanti river that ran through Madore City and wandered on down through the plains, growing wider and more sluggish until it reached the sea.

It was cool under the thick mango trees, cool and dark. They seemed to be riding together in a green tunnel, with the river reflecting back the light that filtered through the leaves, so that watching Sara, riding in her white robes from one patch of shade to another, with the green reflections throwing shadows on her white figure and on her face, Alan was once more enchanted, held inside a circle of happiness because he was with her. Forgetting time, and danger, bemused, he rode behind her to the river's edge, the words of warning he should have said, the quick return he should have insisted on, forgotten.

They came out of the mango grove and into the open, the river sparkling at their feet. Sara swung herself down from Zuleika's back and the mare stretched her neck to drink.

' Is this not beautiful? It is the only green place on the whole plain, except for the garden of the Madoremahal. Do you see the house – there, on the other side of the river? That is an old dâk bungalow. It is built from some of the stone that was left when the Madoremahal was built. The first Ruler – my great grandfather – used to take his girls there, I am told. I often ride down here with Zuleika – I expect that is why she came straight here. She just needed a good run. But it is so lovely here – '

' Very lovely.' Alan was not looking at the river. Sara raised her silver eyes to his briefly and then looked down again, and Alan, lost in his dream, said, ' So lovely – you are so lovely. Sarajan they call you sometimes. What does that mean? Jan? '

' My father added it to my name. It means Soul, or Spirit – '

' What a suitable name. You are like a spirit, a dream – I

37

have never met anyone like you. I shall – I can never forget you – you are like all the women a man dreams of combined into one.'

Her full, enticing mouth smiled a little, but she did not look at him. She ran her hand in a lingering caress down Zuleika's neck and said, 'Major Reid – do you realise we should not be here? They will be looking for us.'

Alan, brought sharply back to reality, was shocked by his own stupidity.

'Great God – I beg your pardon. How long have we been here? Please mount – or would you rather take my saddle?'

'I do not need the saddle. We have only been here about ten minutes. So we have been away half an hour. It will take us about twenty minutes to get back. We are still within the hour Kassim gave my mother. But I am surprised no one has been to look for us. Let us go –'

The sound of men's voices, and horses moving through the grove, came to them clearly. Arrested, they both listened. Was this the search party? Alan knew suddenly that it was not. These people were coming from the direction of the city of Madore. He spoke below his breath.

'Sara, ride for your life back to your home and tell Kassim I am setting a false trail. I will return another way, but if he wants to take you and your mother, do not wait for me. I will find you. Go, Sara – now.'

Without a word, Sara rode off, moving slowly and quietly through the grove. Above the sound of the river Alan could not hear her, and he hoped that the approaching riders would miss her too. He mounted Safed, and set off at a rough trot, talking loudly and making as much noise as he could. He heard shouts behind him, and kicked Safed into as much speed as he could, getting himself into the thickest part of the grove and praying that he would be followed. He heard horses crashing through the undergrowth behind him, but looking over his shoulder he could see no one, the trees were so thick, and the shadows so dark. Presently he found he could hear nothing, so, making a wide detour he turned for the Madoremahal, coming to it on the side where the wall was pierced by the gate. He knocked loudly, and found his own men still on duty.

'The Begum Sahib – the young Begum – has she come through?'

'Nay, Sahib – Wazir the bearer went out, but no one has been through.'

A feeling of disaster came to Alan. He rode fast down the drive, hoping that Sara had come back the way she had gone out – over the hedge and into the stable.

Both Bianca and Kassim were on the *chibutra* – Kassim ran forward to meet him as he reined to a stop.

'Sara?'

'No. Rama and Wazir and Sakhi Mohammed are out – but she has not returned. What in the name of the devil possessed you, Alan, to take her into danger at such a time?'

'I did not. You have not heard what happened? Did Rama not give you my message?'

'He said Sara had jumped the stable fence and you had gone after her – but what kept you so long? You've been out over an hour.'

When Alan had told his story, Kassim looked very grim, and Bianca put her hands up to her eyes. After a minute Kassim took Alan's arm.

'Alan – I cannot go into the city – it will be worse for Sara and Bianca if I get captured, so I shall have to stay here. You must go. Ride to the street of the Metal Workers, it is above the temple – and wait there. If she has been taken, word will be brought to you there – Wazir has gone into the city to ask for news. *If* she has been taken, and you can get her out, do so – but otherwise, come back here – and we will have to plan. Are you armed?'

'I have a knife and a pistol –'

'Don't use the gun if you can avoid it – it merely attracts unwanted attention. Here, take my dagger as well, and Alan, for all our sakes try not to bring any pursuit back here.'

No word of reproach, but Alan rode away feeling like a fool.

Kassim's rage was all the more obvious for being controlled. Alan cantered out through the gate and on to the sunbaked road, knowing that Kassim's rage was justified, and that he had put Sara's life in danger through his own foolishness.

Chapter 6

The city was quiet. Riding through the narrow winding streets
Alan saw that the wooden shutters were down and barred on all
the shops. The covered bazaar was silent behind its iron gates,
and, most ominous sign of all, there were no women to be seen,
There had obviously been a bad riot, and, possibly, another was
expected. He saw one or two men, who did not look at him –
they appeared to be hurrying in the same direction as he was
going, and neither spoke to him or looked his way.

The silence grew deeper, Alan felt the tension mounting. He
was conscious of being watched from behind the wooden shutters
and the barred blind windows. The streets were very narrow as
he got closer to the heart of the city; the houses were mostly built
of wood, with balconies that leaned out over the street, almost
touching over his head. His mare was as uneasy as he was – she
shied violently several times and Alan had to keep her on a tight
rein, for he felt she might easily bolt.

They entered the street of the Metal Workers and the silence
here was so unusual that it was uncanny; this was a place of
constant noise, where all day the street rang with the noise of
hammered metal. Now it was quiet – a strange, listening quiet
– the people behind the shutters, the women behind the barred
windows, were not only watching Alan, they were waiting for
something. Alan now saw no one, and apart from the sound of
Zenobia's hooves striking the beaten earth of the street, it was
so quiet that Alan heard a whisper so clearly that it might have

been a shout.

' Sahib – Sahib ! Do not stop, but go slowly – '

Alan rode on, slowing Zenobia to a jerking, reluctant walk. He could see no one – the speaker must be on one of the balconies, lying behind the carved wooden railings. The whisper came again.

' Sahib, stop at the house with the lotus flowers carved on the balcony screens. Do not dismount – look to your saddle and reins as if something was wrong.'

The House of the Lotus Flowers was well known in Madore. It was the first house in the street of the Harlots and Alan had been there several times, usually with Kassim.

He rode on slowly, and stopped with difficulty beneath the balcony and attempted to examine his girth while Zenobia danced and pulled at her reins. The whisper, when it came, was a woman's sibilant voice.

' Sahib. They have the little Begum. Hardyal has her – in the Temple. There is no time for you to go back – go on, and do what you can, for Hardyal is marrying her before the people, using the old ceremony. You must be quick. Wazir is taken too. Rama I have sent back with the news to the Madoremahal. Now, Sahib, listen carefully. You will not be able to get the Begum out of the temple because of the crowds. Take her further into the temple, and beyond the first courtyard turn left and you will find an old shrine with a goddess dancing. Go behind that figure and slip through the priest's door that is there. Go, Sahib, now – and may the Goddess protect you.'

The sound of urgency in the woman's voice sent Alan and Zenobia into a fast canter. Alan pulled the mare over on to the dust at the side of the road and gave Zenobia her head until he came in sight of Madore Temple.

The square before the temple was thronged. There was no chance of getting near the gates, for all the people of the city seemed to be in the square. The total silence held by such a large crowd was frightening. As one man they were staring up at the dais outside the temple and they did not notice Alan at all

42

they were so involved with what was taking place up there. Alan could hear a priest's voice raised in a monotonous chant, but he could see nothing.

Zenobia was now a liability. There was nothing for it but to let her go. He dismounted, and turning the mare gave her a smart slap on her rump and saw her going fast in the direction from which they had just come. Then he turned and began to work his way slowly to the front of the crowd, feeling as if he was invisible, for no one stopped him. The crowd was one pair of ears and one pair of eyes, a mob completely hypnotised.

When Alan got to the front, and could see the dais which was only twenty yards from the edge of the crowd, he became as still as the rest of the crowd, but he was not hypnotised – he was gathering his forces for what he saw he would have to do.

For Sara was there. She stood beside a tall, broad-shouldered man, and appeared to be unhurt and unafraid. Watching her, Alan wondered if she could have been drugged, her face was utterly expressionless, as still as the face of the stone goddess behind her. There was a small fire burning in a flat iron dish on a tripod. As the priest chanted, he threw something on to the fire and a thick white smoke rose from the red coals. Alan could smell the sweet heavy smell from where he stood. He looked carefully about him, checking to see if there was any way to bring Sara out, but the woman who had whispered her directions was right – the crowd was too thick. It would have to be the plan the woman had told him.

As he looked back at the dais, he saw that standing, heavily bound beside Sara, was the old bearer Wazir, his head bare. There was blood on his white uniform but he stood erect and proud beside his mistress.

The chanting of the priest grew louder and other priests' voices joined in. Another handful of incense was thrown on the fire, and Alan saw Hardyal hand a short rod to the priest, who thrust it into the fire, while the scented smoke thickened and curled round their heads.

In the temple, a deep-toned gong sounded once; the noise

43

vibrated and rang for several minutes, and then silence came back. There was no chanting now. Wazir was grasped by two priests and as he was dragged forward he turned his head, and his voice clear and steady, his eyes on Sara, he said loudly, ' My life for yours, heaven born, now – '

In mid-sentence, a sword swept and Wazir's headless body fell at Sara's feet, his blood splashing up on to her white robes. It was over in a second – Wazir's head rolled like a ball to the edge of the dais, and bumped down the steps, to lie in the dust, while his body jerked and threshed, pumping blood at Sara's feet, until at last it lay still. Sara had neither moved nor looked. Her eyes stared out, over the crowd, as if she could see something far away. Alan knew then that she was drugged, and thanked God for it.

The priest bending over the fire straightened up. Hardyal moved forward holding Sara's hand so that she moved with him. The priest picked up the short rod from the fire, his hand wrapped in a cloth and Alan began to tense his muscles for his planned dash. But he was not prepared for what happened next.

The priest stepped up to Sara and put the white-hot point of the rod he was holding on to her cheek.

Alan's shot took him seconds later and the priest dropped like a stone. Alan rushed up the steps of the dais, almost falling they were so slippery with blood, and while surprise was still on his side he seized Sara before she fell and, running as fast as he could, he carried her straight into the temple. He ran through the first courtyard before he heard any sounds of pursuit – saw the dark shrine on the left, and dashed in. There was a large figure of a goddess, many armed and open mouthed, her tongue protruding, a necklace of skulls round her neck and hanging between her naked breasts. With Sara lying over his shoulder like a sack, Alan ran behind the figure and found himself in total darkness. He felt frantically for the door he had been told was there, and found a slit, barely wide enough to allow a man to slip through. With enormous difficulty he managed to push Sara through, hearing the crowd shouting in the distance and the sound of many people running in the central courtyard. He inched through himself, and found that he was in total darkness and in a very confined space. He backed away to one side of the slit, and holding Sara with one arm, took out his dagger. It would not be long, he felt sure, before the slit door was discovered, and he wondered how long he would be able to hold them off when they came.

The figure that slipped through the narrow door moved so quietly that the first warning Alan had was the sound of another man's breathing close to him. He stood tense, his dagger in his hand, his whole being concentrating on listening. The whisper that sounded was close – he felt breath on his cheek, and brought up his dagger fast. But it met nothing. The whisper came again, from the other side of the slit.

'Sahib – I am a friend. Rama the goat-herd sent me. You must follow me. Take the Begum up, and put your hand on my shoulder. I am taking you down into the vaults.'

Alan was already holding Sara over his shoulder. He heard a faint sound, like a moth moving on a window pane. There was a sudden draught of cold air at his feet, and putting out his hand, he gripped a bare shoulder, then moving with infinite care, began to go down and down a narrow winding flight of stone steps. They seemed to go down a long way, but at last they reached level ground, and the man leading him moved forward, and said, 'Wait here, Sahib, behind this pillar. I close the trap,' and went from under Alan's hand with the ease of a fish slipping through water.

It was completely dark, and Alan could hear nothing. He put Sara down gently, and felt for her pulse. It was light and fast. He could smell the nauseating odour of burned flesh, and wondered desperately how bad her burn was, and what he could do for her with no light, and no medicaments. Suddenly, the place they were in was like a prison. He could not imagine how they would ever get out. He was worried about Sara. When the drug wore off, how could he keep her quiet? And where was the man who had brought them here? Was he really a friend? His last words echoed unpleasantly in Alan's memory – ' I close the trap.'

Oh God, thought Alan, are we trapped? He stood behind the pillar, his mind selecting and rejecting plans, each one seeming more hopeless than the last. He had no idea how long he had been there, he could hear nothing, and there was not the faintest glimmer of light anywhere.

The feet on the stairs were so quiet that the man was almost down in the vault before Alan heard his breathing, and then the faint whispering voice, light as a breath beside him.

' There is a hornet's nest up above. You killed the Chief Priest, the Holy One of the temple. But that was good, for only he knows of this place. This part of the temple is very old – no one comes here any more and it is used as the storehouse for the treasures of the temple. I was told of it by Muna the dancer – she who spoke to you from the House of the Lotus Flowers. Now listen, Sahib. You are to stay quiet down here until we can arrange to get you out. The Begum will not be well enough for two or three days – and also, that will give the hornets above time to settle down a little. I will bring food. There is water at the far end of the vault, Muna says, where the priest used to do ritual cleansing. Here is a small lamp, and tinder – do not keep the lamp here, take it down to the far end – you will find three seated gods there, and behind them is space enough for you, also the water conduit is there. I will return with food and a blanket and some ointment for the Begum's face, and bring you all the news I can. But Sahib – silence and patience.'

Alan found the lamp and the tinder box in his hand and knew himself alone again.

He could not carry Sara through the dark and did not dare to leave her lest she roused and made a noise, so risking it, he lit the lamp and turning it to the merest glowworm spark, picked Sara up and made his difficult way down past chests and rolls, and round great carved pillars to the far end of the vault. The three seated gods were enormous, their faces lost in darkness. He went round behind them, and found that they provided an

46

adequate place of shelter, and that there was a carved fish from the mouth of which dripped water which fell into a marble basin.

He made Sara as comfortable as he could by removing his jacket and rolling it into a pillow for her. She was not conscious. He raised the lamp to look at her cheek and nearly dropped it, her wound looked so dreadful. The burn was a bad one, the flesh round it looked red and angry and the burn looked very deep. It was like a nightmare, one side of her face was perfect, the other a ghastly travesty of what it had been. But at least her eye had been spared. As he looked, her eyes opened and she stared up at him, her eyes slowly focusing.

' Major Reid? What is it? Did I fall? – my face hurts.' She put her hand up, and he caught it just in time.

' No – hush, Sarajan, speak very low. You were burned badly. Can you remember anything? '

' Not very much. I am thirsty.'

' Wait – and please do not touch your face.'

He found a brass cup beside the water spout and brought her a cup of water. As she drank she looked about her, at the shadowed place where she lay, and her eyes were puzzled.

' You are in the temple, Sara – down in the vault. I carried you here. Can you remember anything at all? ' She frowned and an expression of pain and fear twisted her face.

' Yes. I can remember something. I was taken by Hardyal's men and brought to the temple. He – he is horrible. He said he was going to marry me and take the throne of the three States. He said the Ruler, my father, and Kassim were as good as dead – then he gave me something to drink and I woke up here – but *what* is wrong with my face? It hurts very much.'

' Sarajan – the priests branded you – '

' *What!* '

' Yes. At Hardyal's orders, I think. I came in time to stop the marriage – and shot the priest. Don't worry, soon we will have a plan to get out of here – but we have to wait until you are a little stronger, and it has quietened down up above in the temple.

47

They are hunting for us now.'

She shuddered, and he put his hand out and took hers.

' Will you promise me something? '

' What, Sarajan? '

' If they catch us – will you kill me before Hardyal gets me? Promise? '

' They are not going to catch us again,' said Alan firmly.

' Yes, but if something goes wrong, and they do – will you promise to kill me? ' She stared keenly up at him and then sighed, and said sadly, ' You cannot promise because you know you will not do it.' Alan was silent, and at last she said, ' Then will you give me a knife, so that I can do it – myself? '

There was the sound of a footfall on the other side of the Great Gods and before Alan could move, Sara had sat up, and snatched Kassim's dagger from his belt. She had it at her breast when the figure of a young man in a loin cloth, his combed hair hanging on brown polished shoulders came round the side of the gods and stood looking down at them.

' Softly, Begum Sahiba, I am a friend. I will promise you, you will never be taken alive by that swine; indeed, I trust you will escape. But should all go wrong, then I myself will ensure that you are dead before he gets you. Now rest, and let me look at your face. Muna has sent you ointment and I am to apply it straight away; also I have a herbal drink for you. My name is Mistri.'

Deftly, gently, the ointment was smeared on Sara's ruined cheek. Mistri went away to another part of the vault and came back with a bundle of grey duffle robes, and he helped Sara to put one of them on, and then made up the others into two makeshift beds. Rolled in the blanket he had brought, Sara swallowed the draught he gave her, and lay back.

' Muna,' she said. 'Muna – who is Muna? '

' Muna, the dancer – she is very famous – and very beautiful.'

' Muna the dancer – Munabhen – '

' Munabhen? Why do you call her that? ' asked Mistri – but Sara, lying back in her blanket did not answer. She was asleep.

'Thank the goddess for that. She must have been in terrible pain and fear. Why did you not promise to kill her, she was so afraid of being taken by Hardyal again. He is a monster.'

'I could not kill her – kill Sara?'

'You would rather see her taken by Hardyal?'

'I would fight to prevent it.'

'And if you failed?'

'I would kill myself –'

'And leave her to bear all that she would have to bear. Well, well.' Mistri shook his handsome head. 'You English are strange people.' He turned to rummage in a bundle.

'Here, Sahib – food. There is vegetable curry and chapattis. Eat well. I have more here for the Begum if she wakes hungry. But I think that she will eat nothing more than milk when she wakes. That burn will give her much pain.'

They both looked over at Sara, lying so still; her colour had faded to a drained yellow, her eyelashes lay on her cheek in black half moons. The ointment was thick and green and completely hid the burn. Poor beautiful Sara. Alan felt as if his heart would break as he looked at her.

Mistri spoke into his thoughts: 'Sahib, we think we can get you out in four days. Listen. It will be a good night for us to escape, for it is the big festival of the year. Already the hill priests and those from the south are coming in, and the temple will be full of strangers. In four days' time, no one will be able to tell who comes from where. Also, they have quietened down above, and are busy choosing the next Chief Priest. Only Hardyal is trying to keep up the search. The others have lost interest – the late Chief Priest was not beloved – I will see Hardyal tonight, and come in tomorrow evening with news. There is enough food here for you till then, and more ointment, which must be applied when the Begum wakes. There is milk here, and Cognac. Sahib, I will have to leave you. Be quiet and patient – and Sahib, for pity's own sake, leave her the dagger. I think she will die of fear if she thinks she cannot defend herself against Hardyal. But tell her – tell her that Hardyal will

49

be very occupied for the next twelve hours : she will understand.'

Like a wind dropping on a hot day, Mistri was gone, with no sound. Alan realised that when he did let himself be heard, it was because he wished to warn them.

He turned back to Sara and saw her still sleeping, half her face green and glistening, the other half sallow but perfect. Kassim's dagger was held closely in her hand, as a sleeping child will hold its mother's hand. Alan looked at her a little longer, and then pulled his bed over close to hers, turned the lamp down to a mere glimmer, and propping himself up against the wall, prepared to watch through whatever time of day or night it was. He had forgotten to ask Mistri what time it was – he had said he would see Hardyal ' tonight ' – did that mean it was morning outside now? He reckoned that it had been late afternoon when he had brought Sara down to the vaults, but had no idea how long he had been down under the temple. He sat, with the glowworm light, and tried to keep awake, while the shadows of the vault moved about him and the water conduit dripped and splashed into the marble basin.

Chapter 7

Alan must have slept.

He woke to darkness, and the sound of movement, and putting out his hand, found Sara's blanket empty.

' Sara.'

Soft as his whisper was, she heard and answered immediately.

' I am here – but do not come. I have to be alone for a few minutes. I do not need the lamp, it went out a while ago. I will speak again, and when you answer me, I will come back.'

He heard her moving further away. The lamp and the tinder box were close to his hand, and he held both ready, waiting for her voice. When she spoke his name, he lit the lamp, and turning it low, went round the gods to meet her.

' I fear I am sacrilegious – but nature is a force not to be denied.' To his amazement he heard laughter in her voice, and imagined how the average English girl would have behaved in similar circumstances. He thanked God for her natural attitude and led her back to her nest of duffle robes.

' I shall now go and be sacrilegious – and when I come back, I shall give you some milk.'

She refused the milk on his return, however, and asked for water instead. In the dim glow of the lamp, her face looked terrible. Half of it was very swollen, the burn appeared to have turned purple and to be pushing through the green ointment in a monstrous swelling. Alan remembered that he had to put more ointment on her face – he told her so, and she turned her

51

terrible cheek to him, and as he dipped his finger into the strong smelling green stuff, she watched him sidelong and saw the repugnance in his face. She was very quiet after that. He told her of Mistri's plan for their escape, and she nodded.

'I am perfectly all right. I will practise walking a little more today. I seem unsteady on my feet.' When Mistri came hours later, he found Sara and Alan walking slowly up and down the vaults. They went back to their hiding place and he looked at Sara.

'I am happy, Begum Sahiba, to see you so well. May I look at your face?'

Sara sat obediently, her eyes closed, while Mistri bent over her, holding the lantern close. She flinched a little when he laid a gentle hand on her chin to turn her cheek to the light. For a long moment he frowned at the great purple lump that was forming on her cheekbone, pushing her left eye closed, but his voice was calm when he said, 'Muna's salve works well. Come, we will try a little more. She told me to be sure and keep the burn covered with the salve. Does it hurt you?'

Sara shook her head, and Mistri scooped up a great dollop of the green ointment and plastered it all over her cheek.

'Now, Begum Sahiba – lie down and rest. Have you eaten anything? No? Then I have curds and honey for you – eat them, and I have the herb drink you had yesterday. You will sleep and gain as much strength that way as you will by walking about. Your unsteady feet are caused by the drug you were given by Hardyal – that should have left your body by tomorrow.'

After she had eaten a little, and had swallowed the draught from the silver cup, she fell asleep almost at once. Mistri had brought more oil for the lamp. He filled it, and turned to Alan.

'Come, Sahib. We talk. Leave the lamp low, beside the Begum, and we will not, I think, disturb her if we sit here.'

His shoulders shone like polished marble, his dark hair curled to meet them. He stretched his long slim legs out beside Alan, his loin cloth so white that it seemed to glow in the semi-darkness.

'Well, Sahib, Hardyal is determined that you and the Begum

are still somewhere close – he has had bands of his creatures searching the temple, but this is beginning to annoy the priests, and so he will have to call them off. Also I think my efforts have taken his mind off you for the time being. Ooof, it is indeed hard work. That man is everything that is evil.' He sighed, and stretched and a strong smell of musk and roses came from his body.

At that moment it came to Alan that Mistri, the beautiful boy, was in fact one of the people that Alan had, all his life, loathed and despised – a catamount, a male prostitute, a lover of men – abnormal, horrible. All these thoughts ran through his head as he stared at the body beside him, scented, delicately boned – a boy's body, with a boy's face, the lazily smiling eyes half veiled as Mistri looked back at him.

' Well, Sahib – you look at me strangely. Is something wrong? '

This boy, certainly no more than seventeen, had fed and looked after them, risking his life – and was now using his body on their behalf. Alan shook his head and smiled straight into the tired young face opposite.

' Nothing is wrong, Mistri, my friend, except that I have no way to say thank you – '

' I can think of several ways, Sahib, but none of them I fear would appeal to you. Sad, but no matter.' There was a sly side of laughter in his voice, but he sobered quickly.

' I shall come with robes for you both tomorrow. We are going out in the guise of hill priests. Tomorrow evening, just at sunset. Hardyal will be, I trust, sleeping. I wish you to come up the steps and wait in the priest's room. We will robe ourselves there and be able to get out quickly. There is a small spy hole to the left of the slit by which you entered, and you can see into the outer courtyard through it. Let the Begum rest all day tomorrow, for she will need strength. Muna will take her out first, over the wall, and then, when she is safe, we go out by the gates, there will be so much coming and going no one will notice us.'

' Can you tell me the time? – my watch has stopped and I have no way of knowing what time it is down here – I do not know if it is night or morning.'

'When I came down it was eight hours of the night. I think I have been here an hour – if your timepiece works, then if you make it nine hours, it should be right. You have been here already three days.'

'Is that all? It seems like three weeks.'

'Time passes slowly in the empty dark, although you have the Begum to care for. Now. Listen carefully. Take the Begum up at six hours by your watch. It will be light enough to see when you get up there – and you will hear the temple gong ring the hour before sunset if you are there – you can hear nothing down here. Now come with me while I show you how the trap works.'

He led Alan up the winding stair and shone his light on the face of a grotesque demon. 'Put your hand here, Sahib, on his left eye, and push – gently. I have oiled the hinge. There will be no sound. There, you have it now. Let me take you down.'

Back in the vaults, Mistri handed the light to Alan. 'Sahib. I must go – for all our sakes it is necessary that I am at Hardyal's side when he wakes. How fortunate we are that, unlike you, his tastes run in my direction. Women do not always interest him, except for what they bring him – like the emerald Peacock and a throne –'

'The emerald Peacock?'

'You do not know about it? Then if the Begum is wakeful, you can ask her about it – she can tell you. Sahib, rest and gather your forces. We will need all our wits and all our strength tomorrow. Please all the gods, tomorrow night you will be safely out of here.'

He stood up, and walked out of the circle of lamplight, making no sound.

Alan found himself left with the scent of musk and attar of roses, and a feeling that he had been talking to a very brave man.

Sara slept deeply, so still that Alan bent over her to make sure that she still breathed. The green ointment completely covered one cheek, and he could not see if the burn was any better.

He could not sleep. He felt that each minute was as long as a year. He sat, wondering how on earth Mistri expected to get them out. His thoughts flew from one fearful possibility to another, like bats in the dark. When he finally came to the thought that Mistri could easily betray them, he could no longer sit still, but got up and paced about and, to his regret, woke Sara. But she seemed refreshed and asked for food, and ate some of the curds and honey that Mistri had left for her. While she was eating, Alan recalled Mistri's words, and asked about the emerald Peacock.

' It is our State emblem. While the Ruler lives it never leaves his possession – who holds it, holds the throne of Lambagh and rules the three States. It is, I suppose, like your Queen's crown – the emblem of Royalty and Rulership. It is very old – a chain of emeralds, ending in one big stone, carved into the shape of a Peacock with a spread tail. Who told you about it? '

' Mistri. Just before he went. Sara, we are to escape tomorrow night.' He told her the details of the plan, and said, staring into the darkness beyond the guardian gods, ' I hope to God we can trust him, Sara.'

Sara, sitting with one hand shading her cheek, shrugged her shoulders.

' He has had three days in which to betray us, and has not done so. I think that he loves Rama so much that he includes us into his love, as if we were Rama's family – '

' Rama? The goat-herd? '

' Yes. Did you not know? Mistri is Rama's lover, and Rama is his. They are both from Lambagh, and have been lovers for about a year now. They love each other very deeply.'

Her calm acceptance of the situation bereft Alan of words, but Sara did not appear to notice. She went on speaking softly.

' I have been thinking, Alan. Even if we are captured we will not be killed, or harmed. I, because I am too important to Hardyal, and you – well I do not think they will dare to harm you, your regiment must already be searching for you.'

No, thought Alan, no – they will not be looking for me, nor

for Kassim. They think we are on a shooting trip together. He did not say this to Sara, however. He noticed that she was lying quiet again, obviously exhausted. Where would she find the energy and strength she would need for the escape? These four long days of captivity, the lack of comfort and proper treatment of her wound, must have taken a great deal of strength from her, in spite of her youth. Her face seemed less swollen, but she would not let him examine it, keeping her hand over it and her head turned away, and assuring him that the wound no longer hurt her.

The long night and the long day passed, with Sara sleeping a little and then waking to ask for drinks of water. Alan peered at his watch so often that when at last he saw it was almost six, it took him by surprise.

They came out from behind the three great figures, the lantern making a little path of light ahead of them. Alan looked back and the three gods seemed to be watching them go with blank, uninterested eyes.

It took Sara a long time to climb the stairs, and it was just after six when they entered the priest's room. Alan peered through the little spy hole – it was growing dusky in the courtyard. Mistri should have been there. Sara, sitting against the wall, seemed to be sleeping. Alan sat down near her, positioned so that he could see through the slit doorway into the courtyard, and prepared to wait for Mistri with as much patience as he could muster.

Chapter 8

It was Sara who stayed awake.

She roused Alan from the sleep that overtook him.

'I hear one coming,' she said under her breath. 'Not Mistri, Alan – someone else.'

He put her behind him, and took his knife in his hand. If Mistri had betrayed them, then this would be one of Hardyal's creatures – and he found that the four days in the vaults had left him weak and stale. He felt terror that he would not be able to defend Sara.

'Begum Sahib – Sahib – do not be afraid. I am Rama –'

'Rama!'

The shock of relief made Alan lean back against the wall and Sara took his arm.

'Alan? Are you well?'

'Yes – only relief on top of fright. I thought it was treachery approaching. Rama, thank God it is you – but where is Mistri?'

'He waits outside, near the gate, to give us a signal. He has his flute, and when we hear him play we go at once, through the gate. Put on these robes – Sahib, you must take off your clothes and throw them back down the steps and wear these –'

In the half dark Alan stripped and put on a pair of loose native trousers and a shirt. Over this went the duffle robes of a hill man. Sara was already dressed, her head bound closely in a dark cloth, and they were ready to go. Alan kept his knife in his hand, Sara put a fold of her head cloth over her mouth, and they slipped out one by one through the narrow door, walking round the figure of the dark dancing goddess with her necklace of skulls. Then they were out in the sweet evening air of the temple garden. Even the dusk of the early evening was dazzling, after the total darkness they had lived in for so long. Alan had to screw his eyes up to clear them.

Bushes and pillars and the smell of flowers, and the sight of the early evening stars – it seemed unbelievable that freedom was within reach.

Rama moved fast, and they hurried with him. Presently they came round a corner and up to a small pavilion, half in ruins, and Rama put up his hand to halt them.

' In there.'

They went in and, crouching behind a crumbling wall, looked out at a clear view of the gate, and a figure leaning negligently against it, talking to a man who sat on a string bed, with a curved sword and rifle across his knees.

' That is one of Hardyal's men – the priests do not guard the temple gates.'

The man was not particularly alert. He was sitting back, and the mouthpiece of his hookah was in his hand – they could hear the soft bubbling as he smoked. Rama put his mouth close to Alan's ear.

' Mistri has a drug – he will put it on the charcoal of the hookah, and the guard will sleep. Then we go – so be ready.'

They watched, straining their eyes, and saw how Mistri strolled over and sat on the bed beside the guard, taking turn and turn about with the hookah. They saw the guard's attention diverted, and Mistri's hand move with the speed of a striking snake. The guard took the mouthpiece of the hookah from him, took a deep pull, and seconds later fell forward, sliding until he lay on the ground, Mistri deftly catching his weapons before they could clatter down. With an easy push of his foot Mistri rolled the guard out of sight under the bed, and sat down in his place, the weapons across his knees. He took up his flute and played, music that sounded like drops of water, falling into a full cisten. Alan and Rama were on their feet, pulling Sara with them.

' Walk to the gate, and out – do not run.'

In single file, they went towards the gate and saw Mistri's mouth smile behind his flute. They crossed an open space, and were close to the gate when Rama stopped. Mistri put his flute down slowly and sat upright, looking out through the gate, his face expressionless, and Rama dropped back beside Alan.

' Walk on. Go past the gate and round the wall – do not hurry, and do not stop until you come to a thorn tree growing close against the wall. Shelter there and wait for us.'

Disaster. With Sara following him, Alan walked on, grateful for the deepening dusk. They passed the gate and Alan saw a band of horsemen coming up towards them. The leader he could not mistake. Hardyal.

It was hard to walk so slowly, but he forced himself to continue at what seemed a snail's pace.

He could hear Rama speaking loudly to Mistri.

' Ho, Mistri – this is a strange duty for you?' and Mistri's reply :

' I take the place of Darsu who has gone to the privy. May the gods protect all of us if I have to fire this thing – I shall die of fright.'

' And so shall I – just keep still until Darsu returns.'

There was the sound of a horse cantering in, and Rama's voice again.

' Well, Mistribhai, I shall leave you in case you move the wrong finger. Do you come to the Street tonight? Perhaps we will meet there.' As he spoke he was moving, for his voice sounded further away. Alan and Sara strolled on, and suddenly a voice shouted behind them, cracking with rage.

' Wait – you ! I know you – you come from the Madoremahal. What do you do here? Stop, or I shall fire – and not to kill. I want answers to some questions – stop – '

Depite himself, Alan turned, and Sara quickly pulled him into the shadow of the wall.

' Alan – wait – there is nothing you can do.'

' I can't leave Rama – '

' You can only endanger him – wait –'

Alan could not see Rama, but Hardyal was off his horse and aiming his rifle.

Mistri moved then and, standing, he raised the rifle, pointing it directly at Hardyal. Alan heard his voice.

' Do not shoot, Nawabsahib – for you will be a dead man if you do – '

The whole scene seemed frozen for a moment. Hardyal, his rifle in his hands, staring at Mistri, Mistri standing, his rifle a foot from Hardyal's body.

The bullet that was fired from the gate was fired by a marksman. Mistri dropped like a stone, lying on the ground in front of Hardyal's horse, and a darker shadow began to grow round his head. There was only the sound of a single loud sob, like a child might make, waking frightened in the dark, and a deep sigh, and then silence.

The silence did not last long. It was broken by a perfect fusillade of shots. Hardyal's men appeared to be firing in all directions at once, as if the first shot had been a signal. Some bullets sang past Alan, and he took Sara's arm and pushed her in front of him, keeping his body between her and the men behind.

' They are only spent bullets – they are not firing at us, they cannot see us, so do not be afraid, Sarajan.'

His whispered encouragement was immediately proved wrong. All the bullets were not spent. Alan felt a hard blow on his arm just below the shoulder, and then a searing pain. He heard Sara gasp, and half turn towards him, and thought savagely, ' Christ – not now! I cannot be wounded now.' He felt deathly sick and turned quickly to bend his head to his knees to fight off the faintness that was threatening to overcome him. As his head cleared, and he straightened, he had only one thought – to get Sara to the thorn tree Rama had spoken of as quickly as possible. What they were going to do there, if Rama did not come, he had no idea.

Keeping close in the shadow of the wall, he hurried Sara, unable to help her when she stumbled, because he was clutching his arm, where he could feel blood spreading warm over his fingers. Sara was moving fast, and had made no further sound; he hoped that she had not realised that he had been shot, as it would add to her fears, which must already be great.

He saw the thorn tree and at last drew Sara in beside its sheltering branches. It was dry and dead and twisted, and would afford little help in scaling the wall, as each twig bore thorns about two inches long and as sharp as dagger points. The wall loomed above them, impossibly high, the top sparkling even in the growing dusk with a thick covering of broken glass and metal points. They both leant back under the thorn tree's sheltering branches and while Alan attempted to stem his own blood from welling out, he looked at Sara. She seemed utterly exhausted, her head back against the wall, her eyes closed. Alan was able to take the cloth that was bound round his waist, and one-handedly tie it below his wound, which he found, after some rather painful investigation, to be only a flesh wound. The bullet had passed clean through the fleshy part of his upper arm. The tightly bound cloth stopped the bleeding and still Sara had neither moved nor opened her eyes. She looked very drawn and shocked, and remembering her courage and calmness in the vaults he was surprised, until he realised that seeing Mistri killed must have been terrible for her. He took her hand, and found it very cold.

' Sarajan, are you all right? '

She opened her eyes and looked back down the way they had come.

' Listen, Alan, someone is coming.'

It was Rama and he was moving fast, not quite at a run. He ducked under the branches beside them and spoke in a harsh breathless whisper.

' Mistri is dead. My friend has left me, dying to save me. May I find him again on the wheel of life, before too long. This

61

world will be a cold and empty place without him, my beloved companion.'

The silence after his words was alive with his sorrow. Then, from the temple came the deep note of a gong.

Rama turned at once to Sara.

'Begum Sahiba, we use the second plan. You go over the wall. The girls will have heard the shooting and will be waiting for you. Just beyond this thorn tree, you go over, and you will be taken to a place of safety where we will join you. All that you have to do is to move fast over the wall. You are ready?'

Before Sara could reply, a band of hill men came round the corner, and up the path towards them, priests, from the southern hills, the country beyond Pandu.

'Stand steady. They know nothing. If we are still, they will not look at us.'

It was hard to stay still. The men were wild-looking creatures, long haired, with tilted, slit eyes, wearing thick felted robes belted about their waists with rope. They stopped not a yard from where Alan stood beside the tree, so close that he could smell their rankness, a combination of sour milk, sweat, and rancid oil. They were looking about them, and Alan was rigid with fear of discovery, but they did not come nearer. There was a very old altar under the wall, the image of the god so worn that it appeared to have no features; it was this for which they had searched. One of them produced a chicken, and they sacrificed it, calling on their god. Then they moved on, leaving the chicken, headless, still flopping about on the altar stones. Rama said, 'Thanks be to all the gods – we must go now.' Alan turned to Sara, and then looked at the wall. 'Sara, can you do it?' She nodded, with no certainty, and he felt a fierce impatience with her. Was all this danger, and Mistri's death, to go for nothing because she had lost her courage at the last minute?

'Come, I will help you up –'

'No, wait, there is broken glass and bits of old knife blades set in the top of the wall – I need something to cover my hands –'

Alan almost snarled at her in rage. 'There is nothing – we

have nothing here – '

' We have,' said Sara quietly. With a quick movement she had thrown off her robe, and stood, a slim figure, stark naked in the dim light. Then, her robe bunched round one hand and arm, she turned to the wall and said, ' Help me, Alan.' Her skin under his hands was like warm silk. With a mind blank of all thought except an astonishment at the softness of her skin, and the fine muscles moving under his hands, he started to try to lift her so that she could reach the top of the wall.

His left arm was, he discovered, almost useless, and Sara did not seem to be as nimble as he had thought she would be. She slipped, missed her grasp at the top of the wall, and fell back into his arms, giving him a jolt of pain that turned him giddy and sick. Where had Rama gone when he was most needed?

' Oh, Alan – hurry – I can hear people coming.'

Pain and irritation at his own disability gave Alan strength he did not know he possessed. Gritting his teeth, he seized her and literally threw her up to the top of the wall, as he would have thrown a sack. He saw her clutch the wall where she had thrown her robe, and drag herself up, one-handed. As she did so, he heard what she had heard – men, walking fast, their feet slapping hard on the paving of the temple cloisters.

These men were not simple hill priests. They were the militant priests of the temple, searching, and they represented trouble. Alan watched them methodically beating the bushes as they approached, with a sick feeling of despair. There was Sara, on the top of the wall, clear against the sky – they could not avoid seeing her.

Rama was suddenly beside him.

' Follow me, Sahib – *now.*'

Alan, giving up everything for lost, saw Rama dart forward to the shadows round the old altar. A diversion to draw attention from Sara? He mentally shrugged. There was no hope that they would not be discovered – for one thing, he must have left a trail of blood behind him – he went after Rama, and Rama, who had the dead chicken from the altar in his hands, grabbed at

Alan's shoulder and pushed him down, and went back to the altar. A high, eerie chant rose from the shadows where he stood, and Alan, kneeling where Rama had pushed him, saw suddenly what Rama was planning, and began to join in the chanting with all his voice.

Never was an altar served by more enthusiastic priests – Alan raised his voice in a wordless chant, as high and nasal as he could make it. Rama sprinkled blood impartially on himself, the altar, and Alan.

The searching priests stopped and looked at them. It would have been impossible to ignore them, their worship was so frenzied. Alan turned his back on them and prostrated himself before the altar. To his horror he saw that Rama had turned towards them – was he mad?

Alan lifted his head, tensing his muscles for battle, and could not help glancing at the top of the wall. It was empty. Sara had gone.

The rush of relief he felt was too much. All his body went limp, and he lay flat, stretched out before the altar, unable to move, a worshipper in a coma.

Rama was unconcernedly collecting sticks, moving here and there among the shadows. The priests had walked on, and were prodding among the bushes, their attention entirely on the ends of their long iron-shod sticks. They had not so much as glanced at the wall. Alan dragged himself to his feet, and Rama brought his bundle of sticks over.

'Start to pluck the chicken,' he said. Alan's astonished stare brought a hurried explanation.

'The sacrifice has been made. Now we must light a fire, cook the bird and eat it. They are all about us – so we must seem to be here as of right.'

Alan saw now that another band of men had joined the first, spoken with them for a few minutes, and were coming down the path towards him. He turned away and began industriously plucking at the bird, bending low over his work. Rama was striking flint and steel. A man, armed with a long curved sword, came and stood beside him. Rama, bending over his fire of sticks, blew hard on the tinder, and smoke billowed out. The tall priest stepped back.

'Hast thou seen anyone running this way – two men, and a girl?' The smoke rose in a cloud, and he coughed, turning away his head. Rama answered him from the smoke, his face completely hidden.

'Nay, we have been here since sundown, and have seen no one, honoured sir. We made our sacrifice and now we will eat.'

The priest turned away, wiping his eyes as the acrid smoke of burning feathers grew thicker.

'Ugh, what worshippers come to our festivals now – flesh-eaters – ' He went off at a trot to join his companions.

It seemed to Alan that his life had been spent squatting in the smoke, plucking the still warm chicken, and watching the searching bands running through the gardens of the temple. The last light had gone, and night was on them, when once more a gong sounded within the temple, and presently, except for the guarded gates, the temple gardens were quiet.

Rama was apportioning the half-cooked chicken as calmly as if this was all he had to do. Alan's desperate impatience shook in his voice.

'How do we know the Begum is safe – where *is* she?'

'The Begum is safe. We would have heard the outcry if she had been captured. As to *where* she is – I hope, getting help of some sort for us. There will be horses waiting by the river if all goes well. As soon as we have eaten, we must go.'

'Eaten? I cannot eat. As for going, how do we go? The gates are still guarded.'

Rama's reply was calm and unruffled. 'The way will be opened, Sahib – be patient. See how all things have worked well for us, since Mistri made sacrifice for us.'

Alan heard the grief in his voice and thought that at least Sara was out of the temple, and please God, alive and safe.

Rama's voice, with its new harshness, broke into his thoughts. 'Which of you was wounded? The path was spattered with blood. I cleared it up as I came.'

' I was – a flesh wound in the arm. I have bound it up.'

' Does it still bleed? No? Good. We have no time to see to it now. We will deal with it when we get out.'

The calm certainty in his voice suddenly gave Alan great confidence. They *would* get out. Sara *was* safe. Mistri's sacrifice would not be in vain.

Chapter 9

The wall, with its sparkling top of broken glass shards and metal pieces, was, to Sara, like a mountain peak, so high that the lights in the windows of the houses on the other side of the narrow street seemed much further away than the stars. She could put up a hand, she felt, and pick the stars from the sky like flowers. She crouched dizzily on the wall, and the lights in the windows dimmed and went out – or were they still there? Her shoulder hurt her very much, as it had done ever since she had felt that sudden blow from behind and Alan had told her not to be afraid, they were only spent bullets. Feeling the warm trickle running down her arm, she knew, muzzily, that she must have been hit by a spent bullet. Her arm was stiff and useless.

But worse than anything was the vertigo that made the whole dark world slide and whirl around her, while the stars grew brighter, and slipped sideways across the misting sky. She crouched lower on the wall and felt the broken glass cutting through the folds of the robe she was sitting on. She remembered Rama's words, ' Move fast over the wall.' Well, she was on the wall, alone and swinging in a swinging world, and she could do no more.

Below her, in the temple precincts and beyond, there seemed to be a great deal of noise – shouting and the sound of running feet. So, she thought calmly, it will all soon be over. I shall be recaptured and that will be a great deal better than sitting on this wall, alone and in pain, stuck between heaven and earth, while the stars play and dance around me to some music that I cannot hear.

It was the wind off the river, the evening breeze, blowing cold on her naked body that saved her – that, and a voice that called softly from the street below – a voice she knew, it seemed, that said insistently, ' Sara – Sarajan – jump. Jump now, we are here.' The wind revived her, the voice gave her confidence. Forgetting her shoulder and her fears, Sara jumped from the wall, dragging her robe with her.

She fell soft, a jumble of arms and legs, into a quilt spread and held to receive her. The jar of landing hurt her shoulder terribly and the stars took a final twirl over the skies and grew enormous, and Sara lost her senses.

There was the familiar scent of jasmine, and cold stone under her feet when she came to herself. For a moment she thought she was back in the garden of the Madoremahal – then found that she was standing stark naked in a street, held upright by one woman outside a closed door where another woman was fumbling with the latch.

The door opened into a dimly lit room, an oil lantern making the shadows seem darker. There was a string bed in one corner, and a girl holding a bundle of clothes. The smaller of the two women who had come in with her said, ' I go, Rhada, and dress – in case of trouble.' Rhada nodded, and led Sara over to the bed. She looked at Sara's shoulder and told the girl to give her some clean rags.

' She is bleeding – badly. We must stop the flow.'

As they bent together over Sara, a burst of drunken male laughter sounded from behind a door on the other side of the room.

' Let us hope Savita can hold him a little longer – and that Muna comes back quickly.'

The woman called Rhada breathed the words like a prayer, but as she spoke, the door was flung open and a man stood swaying in the square of bright light. He was very drunk, but not quite drunk enough, and his eyes widened on Sara's naked body, and dark tangled hair. Rhada tried to stand between Sara and the man at the same time that the girl with her tried to twitch a quilt over her, but the man was already close to them, reaching for Sara's uncovered shoulder and roaring, half in rage and half in amusement.

' So. The sweet meat is kept for others, and I have the old shoe leather? Oh no, Rhada, not so. I will have this one, and more wine and the upstairs room – '

Rhada knocked his hand away and spoke firmly.

' Nay then, breaker of hearts. This one is new, and still drugged, and will not pleasure you tonight. But Muna – she has been listless, longing for you ever since your last visit. Take Muna to the upper room with your wine tonight – and tomorrow when this one has thrown off the effects of the drug, perhaps then you can have the pleasure of breaking in the new colt.'

As she spoke, Muna hurried in, her clothes were red, and she seemed to Sara to dazzle and burn with gold and scarlet, like a flame. She was laughing as she came in, and her swift movement threw back her gauze veil from her head, showing her long black hair, with jasmine flowers bunched at her ears.

' Oh *so*. My beautiful bull – you cast eyes at the little she calves now, do you? Is your strength no longer equal to loving a woman grown, that you lust after children? '

She stood in front of the man, her hands set on her hips, her head thrown back arrogantly as she laughed at him, catching a pointed red tongue between little white teeth at the end of her laughter.

' You long for green apples, oh fool. See, try the apples of gold that are ripe and yours for the taking.'

With a swift movement she pulled at her short tight bodice, tearing it open and baring opulent, pointed breasts, their tips painted with gold – then she tossed her head back and laughed in the man's face.

' But perhaps you are no longer able to deal with rich goods. Fuddled with drink, and weak after your journey. No matter. There are others.'

69

She moved closer to him, until her breasts were just touching his chest, and said softly, ' Oh yes, my friend – there are others. I see I was a fool to waste my time waiting for an old man who likes green girls.'

Her laugh was like the screech of a Peacock. She eluded his suddenly grasping hands and ran out through the door, and the man turned and lumbered after her, Sara forgotten.

' Thanks be to the goddess. Come now, Begum Sahiba – can you walk? We must get you away from here, and have your wound dressed. Sahiba – oh may the goddess aid us – she faints. I will carry her, and you follow with the clothes, and the rags – and hurry. The moon is an hour from rising and they will not be able to wait after moonrise – it will be too light.'

Sara knew nothing of her journey, swaying over Rhada's shoulder, up the rickety stairs, out through a window and over one balcony to another, over the flat roofs of two more houses and down into a room on the ground floor of yet another house. She came back to reality when they dressed her wound, because it hurt her considerably. At her indrawn breath, Rhada said, ' Ah, Begum Sahiba – you are with us again. See, your shoulder is bound up, and now we must dress you. Sit, little Begum, and we will comb back your hair.'

Sara felt that she had come back into the world after many years. Nothing could be normal, she had been away so long. ' Never mind my hair – tell me of my mother – where is she, is she well? '

Rhada looked into the tear-filled eyes. ' Rest, Begum Sahiba. Your mother is well and waits for you in a place of safety. Now sit, and let us order your hair and face.'

' And Goki? '

' The old one? – she is with your mother. She sent you many messages, and will come back and torment us if we send you back to her looking as you do. Please, Begum beloved, let us clean your face at least – we have not much time.'

Sara at length submitted and stayed quiet while Rhada cleaned her face gently. She had forgotten the brand on her cheek in the greater pain from her shoulder, and did not notice Rhada's shocked pause as the dirt and ointment washed away and displayed the star-shaped puckered wound, still purple and inflamed. Rhada said nothing but her face was very sad as she gently dried the small marked face, and then dressed Sara in a *choli*, like the short tight-fitting bodice she wore herself, and the long full skirt that the peasant girls wore. She drew a cloth over Sara's tangled hair and said, ' There – that will do for the present. Now, for a little while, you are one of us. We will drink tea and eat sweet meats and talk until they bring the horses.'

Sara obediently took up the bowl of jasmine-scented tea, holding it carefully between finger and thumb at the very edge as it was so hot, and sipped it. She wondered if Alan and Rama were coming with the horses – surely they were safely out. There were so many questions she was afraid to ask. So she asked one that did not matter.

' Are the girls always drugged when they are new to the houses? '

Rhada stared at her blankly and then she laughed.

' Oho – so you heard that. No, in our houses no girl is ever drugged. We are of those who were vowed to the temple and who have served the goddess gladly. But nowadays some of the other houses take girls who are not willing – and they are drugged. We of the temple despise this very much. We are trained from childhood, and we come freely and gain great merit.'

Her beautiful face, the lamplight playing on it and gleaming on her gold ornaments and earrings, was proud. Sara, with memories circling in her head like bats in a lighted room said, ' Is it never – hard or unpleasant? '

Rhada shrugged. ' Yes, it can be both. You saw Muna tonight. But nothing in life is ever entirely easy and pleasant. There are many wives, tied to the treadmill of children and drunken cloddish husbands, who envy us our lives. We are rich, and free, and admired. So – ' A second shrug finished her sentence.

Sara, between sips asked the first of the questions that were beginning to loom too large in her mind to be ignored. 'Has there been much rioting in the city – has it been bad?'

Rhada's glance at her was sharp, she saw the strained face, the frightened eyes, and answered comfortably, 'Little serious rioting. No one badly hurt. All your people are safe, Begum. Drink your tea – we must go as soon as the horses come because I know the Yuvraj wishes you to leave for Lambagh tonight, provided the Major Sahib and Rama are out –'

So Sara's question was answered before it was asked. All were safe except Alan and Rama – and she was sure that somehow Rama would get them out, and they would all leave for Lambagh at last.

As if the gates of paradise have opened before her, thought Rhada, watching the brightening eyes, the relaxed smiling mouth. Then she sent a curse to whatever devil it was who had branded the girl's face. Poor child, poor little marred one – and yet even so, the Begum managed to look beautiful. Rhada's face, unmarked by line or blemish, had been of such importance in her life that she could only see a disfiguring scar as a major tragedy.

The sound of a horse stamping outside brought Rhada to her feet, and Sara put down her bowl and stood up, biting her lip as her wound throbbed. But she walked to the door unaided and nodded her head firmly when Rhada asked if she was sure she could ride. She waited while Rhada blew out the lamp and drew the bolts on the door, and then the fresh night air came in, and there were the two horses with a man at their heads, a stranger to her, but not to Rhada.

'Sikunder, take the Begum Sahiba up before you – she has been wounded. I will follow. If anyone stops us, she is our daughter, and we are taking her to the Hakim as she has been hurt in the riots.' Sara was lifted in strong arms and held firmly, and Rhada mounted her horse neatly and easily and they moved off at a smart canter.

Sara's arm and shoulder felt as if they were on fire when her horse began to move, but the man holding her shifted his grip and held her so that the jolting was lessened, as he felt her wince.

' My thanks – '

Back came the answer, ' My life for yours, Begum Sahiba,' and she knew that this was a man of Lambagh, one of Kassim's own men, and she felt completely secure.

The darkness of the narrow winding streets gave way to open country, and she felt the air colder, tasting of water. They were riding for the river. The horses gathered speed and she bit her lip now as the pain in her arm and shoulder mounted. Then the pain was past bearing, and once again she saw the wheeling stars sink below the rim of her consciousness. Her head fell forward and Sikunder called out :

' Oh woman, our daughter has fainted. I do not think she can go much further. Stop here, on the bank of the river, keeping in the shadows, and I will go to where our friends wait, and bring them round here with the boat.'

He reined in, and lowered Sara carefully down into Rhada's arms. ' I will take your horse, it will only draw attention that we do not want. Wait in the shadows, here, and I will come back as quickly as I can.'

He turned his horse, and leading Rhada's, galloped off along the edge of the river shallows, and Sara, coming back to consciousness heard only a throbbing like a heart beating, the horses' hoof-beats were so silenced by the mud.

' Rest, Begum Sahiba,' said Rhada, making Sara lie down with her head on Rhada's knees.

' Rest, it is loss of blood that makes you so weak. Sleep a little – Sikunder and our friends will be here soon.'

It was very quiet on the river bank. The stars were no longer wheeling and dancing, they had found their reflections in the dark flowing river, and were still. Rhada's hands were gentle, smoothing back her hair. Sara fell into a light easy sleep, forgetting everything.

73

Chapter 10

Alan and Rama sat back to back, squatting beside the dying fire. Presently Rama got up, and began to heap more brushwood on to the fire and Alan got rid of the bit of half-cooked chicken. The brushwood caught and crackled and a column of flame rose into the thorn tree and began to run, like coloured ribbons, along the dry branches.

'Now, Sahib,' said Rama quietly. 'Follow me, and walk swiftly but do not run.'

Already the thorn tree was crackling like gunfire and smoke was rising and billowing in great clouds as the fire took hold. There were startled cries from a small gate nearby, and the two men who were guarding it came out and stood staring down the path where Rama led and Alan followed.

'Hai – you, what happens down there? You – you men there – what is that fire?'

'Lord, I know not,' said Rama, his voice an unrecognisable whine. 'There are two men, and a girl there, near the wall, they will no doubt put out the fire. I go with Metta Lal to clean the privies of the priests, for thou knowest, it is the hour when the night soil carts come.' He was standing close to the guard now, and the man quickly stepped back to avoid contact with a sweeper, an untouchable of no caste, but he peered at Rama keenly, none the less. Rama ignored him and moved on, passing the gate, calling, 'Come, Metta Lal, come, hurry, I can hear the carts – get the buckets quickly –'

Alan stumbled after him, his breath held in his throat as he went by. The guard was now looking at the fire, and seemed to make up his mind.

' Stay you here, Sitap,' he said to his companion. ' I will go – that fire spreads fast.' He ran off towards the fire, and the other man stood in the path, staring after him and paying no attention to Alan.

Rama went on towards the latrines, followed by Alan. So they were not to try the gate? Rama moved behind the first privy, an odoriferous hut, and said, ' Sahib – climb up, and drop over the other side. I will follow. That fire will have caused a diversion, but also, it will be proof that we are still within the temple walls. So there are things I must do. Wait for me below the wall, and if I do not come within the hour, go to the river.' A shadow among shadows, he was gone.

Alan looked at the wall above him, and as he looked, he realised that the moon had risen. The glass on the wall sparkled cruelly, and he remembered suddenly how Sara had stared up with frightened eyes, and then he took off his robe and tossed it up, and leaped and caught the edge of the wall and felt the glass cutting his hand as he pulled himself up. His arm gave a great burning throb of pain as he half jumped, half fell down the other side, into a narrow, silent lane.

The wait before he saw Rama silhouetted against the sky seemed endless. But at last he was there, and had jumped lightly down.

' Sahib – now we run, as we have strength we run. For they will be after us in minutes from now – '

He was still speaking when he began to run, down a twisting alleyway, and Alan, his cut hand dripping blood and his arm throbbing as if it was being beaten, ran with him.

Rama led him, turning and back-tracking and then turning again, but always heading for the river, and behind them Alan heard the cry of pursuers. Rama paused for a second and Alan heard the dry scrape of tinder and steel – a flame grew and blossomed on the verandah of a wooden house, and they ran on, as startled voices from within the house grew louder and a burst of light rose, behind them.

Rama led them further and further into the darkness and there seemed now to be no sounds behind them, and the lights of fishermen's huts ahead of them. Rama turned away from the huts, and dropped into a walk, and Alan, his lungs bursting and his head whirling, was at last forced to say ' Rama – I can go no further. I will hide here and get my breath.'

' No, Sahib. For all our sakes you must keep on now. Call on whatever gods you worship and move, with me. It is not far now.'

His face in the moonlight was grey and glistening with sweat, and for the first time Alan saw that he was carrying a bundle across his shoulders. He had no breath left with which to ask questions, and they staggered on, until at last the river shone before them.

The moon reflected back from the mud banks and the water. It was silent, and no shouts or cries carried on the wind. An alligator splashed noisily in the shallows at the sound of their coming, and Rama stopped and stood listening for a second, and lowering his burden said barely above his breath, ' It is well, Sahib. Here we wait. They will come for us here.'

Alan dropped where he stood, and lay staring up at the moon and the blurring stars, until the world steadied and his breath came back. He sat up then and began to look about him. They sat among piles of wood. The river was wide here and came close to the shore, the mud flats were narrow and the river flowed swiftly – he could see in the moonlight the arrowing of the midstream current. There was a small wind blowing and the air was fresh, but the smell of smoke and incense seemed to blow with the wind.

Rama was sitting immobile, staring out over the river, his bundle beside him – he looked so solitary, it was as if even his mind was gone, and Alan felt lonely and afraid, so that he spoke louder than he meant to, as if he was calling Rama from a distance.

'Rama!' As if he was returning from far away Rama answered slowly, after a pause.

'Sahib?'

Alan moved a little closer to him. 'What happens now?'

'We wait,' said Rama. 'They will come for us, and for my friend. The fire I lit was a signal.'

Alan stared down at the bundle at Rama's side, and recalled his wait beneath the wall.

'Rama, you went back for Mistri's body – why did you not tell me?'

'You could have done nothing, Sahib. You would have been caught. I knew where they had thrown him so it was easy for me. I could not have left him for the dogs to tear.' He fell silent and then said, 'Also, his mother and his father will wish his burning rites to be correct. For us – well, he is dead, and I am alone. But for them he would be worse than dead if they could not burn him with the proper ceremonies because then his soul would wander, without rest. Perhaps, if that is true, he would have wandered back to me, and we could have spoken together in the long nights. But they will wish to burn him. He sleeps well now, at least.'

He leaned, and turned back a corner of the cloth on the long bundle, and Mistri's face was bared to the moon. Cold, still, and beautiful, the hollows of his eyes secured to hold all the darkness in the world. Alan stared down at him, wordless, remembering how kind and brave he had been – and how young.

Into the silence came the sound of a boat creaking noisily as the oars moved in the rowlocks. Rama stood up.

'They come,' he said, and stepped forward to the edge of the river. At the same time Alan heard the sound of horses, a steady rhythmic beat, unmistakable.

'Rama, I hear horses –'

'It will be the Yuvraj,' said Rama, without turning. 'He has been here every evening, coming from different ways to find if you and the Begum had escaped.'

He turned back to the river, the water no longer silvered by the moon, for a cloud had come over the brightness and suddenly the river was the river of death and a horror, primeval and as paralysing as the feel of a snake's coils round his body, fell from the clouded sky and made Alan gasp, and tremble. What was coming in the boat that had sent such a message along his nerves? A moment before, he had been tired and in pain, and full of pity for Rama and his grief. Now he could think of nothing, could feel nothing but this black despair, worse than fear, a kind of death of the spirit had seized him.

The boat was close and he could see the lantern was being lit – the spark of struck steel and then the slow burning up of the flame, and two figures, one seated, huddled in the prow, the other steadying himself, standing with the lantern held high.

They were old people. An old man, and an old woman – perhaps not old in years, but their faces were seamed with lines that were deepened by the flickering of the lantern, and they looked as old as time. Rama moved slowly down to the water's edge, and helped the boat in, and held it as the woman climbed out. Then the man joined her and they stood, looking up at Rama, and for a moment there was nothing but their staring eyes and the lantern light, and the dark rolled bundle at Alan's feet. The two looked past Rama to Alan, and back again to Rama. Then the man said, ' It is well, you are safe. The boat is here to take you. But my son? When does he come? '

Rama stepped back, and turned, and led them over the mud flats to where Mistri lay, and Alan knew what terrible thing had travelled to him in the boat. Mistri was this couple's son, their hope of immortality, the comfort of their days, and he had died not only for Rama, but also for him, Alan. Nothing he could do would heal the wound dealt to these people, nothing would ever bring Mistri back, or comfort them.

He helped Rama drag wood from one of the piles of firewood and then stood back as Rama uncovered Mistri's body, and he and the father lifted it and laid it on the piled wood. The flask of oil had been brought by Rama and there was no need for the ritual cracking of the skull – the small bullet wound in the forehead had already done that. Rama and Mistri's father went round the pyre, praying, invoking the gods to receive the soul that was soon to be released. The oil was poured and the flame taken from the lantern and put to the dry wood, which caught easily. Rama had brought a paper twist of grains of incense to sprinkle on the pyre and the oil was sandalwood oil. The air was full of sweet scents for the moment. The pyre burned high, and the river was illuminated, even the moon, clear of clouds, faded in the warm red light of the leaping flames.

All this time the woman had stood there, a black shadow a little to one side, a silent watcher. Now, as the flames leapt up and Rama and the father stepped back, she flung away her veil and began to scream. Her cries were horrible, eerie, coming from the uncertain darkness that ringed the firelight. The noise reminded Alan of something – he recalled once in the family lines hearing a woman giving birth. Her screams had been the same. This woman on the shore must have screamed like this when Mistri was born. Now the same cries came from her at his burning. She stood, rigid, her arms cast up over her head, and screamed steadily, one hoarse animal cry after another, until mercifully her throat closed under the strain and she choked and cast herself down on the ground at the foot of the pyre, and broke into bitter sobbing.

Alan found that he had gripped his hands so hard together that his wound had opened again and blood was drenching his sleeve. Rama, who had been standing gazing up and over the flames into the sky, suddenly turned and, coming to Alan, took him by the arm and made him sit, while he retied the makeshift bandage, saying nothing for a while until he had finished. Then he said quietly, ' Sit, Sahib – and do not heed the weeping. Without those tears her heart would break and she would go mad. Tears are a balm and a release.'

Alan wondered what release Rama had, as he looked at the still face of his friend, haloed by the flames, shining like a god's face in the fire.

Chapter 11

Alan was sitting, hunched over his wounded arm, when the steady beat he had heard, at first as quiet as his own heart-beat, grew louder, and changed to heavy thudding, and the horses were suddenly there, two with riders, and one on a leading rope.

So it was that seated he looked up a long way, it seemed, to see Kassim, mounted on a lathered horse, his face in shadow as he drew rein beside Alan.

For a moment, he did not move, looking down at Alan, faceless and eyeless. Then he turned and the firelight flashed in his eyes as he saw the pyre, and the sobbing woman, and Rama standing over the flames beside the old man. He came off the horse in a rush then, and when he spoke, his voice was the voice of an angry stranger.

' Where is Sara – what have you done? '

All the fears and strains of the past few days, and the pain of his wound came together at once in Alan's mind, and Kassim's tone of voice struck a nerve that poured rage all through his body. He stood, rising slowly, to answer Kassim.

' I do not, unfortunately, know where Sara is,' he said, trying to speak slowly and hold his voice steady. ' All I know is that she is out of the temple, and safe.'

' As you are alive and well, I would trust that she *is* safe – for your sake. Rama! ' The snap of command in his voice was a whip that brought Rama's head round at once. Alan, astonished, realised that Rama had not heard the horses come, and that the sight of Kassim was a relief to Rama, even in his deep sorrow.

' Heaven-born, thanks be to the gods. The Begum Sahiba is safe with Rhada and Muna – she will be here before midnight. The pyre – Mistri is dead. He died saving my life, which is worthless.'

' It is not worthless to us, Rama.' Rama joined his hands again, bowed over them, and with a word of excuse went back to the pyre.

Kassim turned back to Alan.

Standing face to face with him, Alan saw that Kassim was in a towering rage, too angry to be able to mask it. Why? His tired mind struggled with the question, and gave up as Kassim spoke.

' Did you make love to Sara?'

' *What* did you say?'

' I asked if you took Sara's body. Is she still a virgin?'

The rage in Alan rose into a great burst of red fury that almost blinded him.

' Mind your own damned business,' he shouted. The two men were so close that Alan could see the reflections in Kassim's angry eyes. He considered Kassim's question to be an abominable slur, both on his honour and on Sara. He half turned away, fighting for control, and turning he saw Kassim's blood-stained turban, and heard the exhaustion in his voice. This was his old friend, a man of different race and creed, a member of Sara's family, and who therefore in eastern custom had a perfect right to question him.

Alan turned back and spoke in a milder tone.

' It seems to you that you have a right to ask that question. No, I did not make love to Sara. In my creed a man does not press his attentions on a young woman when she is in danger and afraid. He guards her honour as he would guard his sister's honour.' What a pompous ass I sound, he thought, angry at the position in which Kassim had placed him.

Kassim stepped back, and sighed, a sigh that moved his whole body, but was almost soundless, as if he had been holding his breath. His expression, what Alan could see of it in the uncertain light, was pitying. Alan's rage mounted again.

'In any case, how dare you ask me that question knowing Sara as you do? Would you have violated her, broken her trust, while she was in danger, afraid, with only you to guard her?'

He flung the words at Kassim, like spears of hatred. Kassim looked quietly at him, his quiet, coming so suddenly after his previous violence, was startling. When he spoke, his voice was its usual lazy drawl.

'Do you mean, would I have made love to her, down there in the long shadowed days and nights when we would not have known what was to come to us, or even if we had a future? Oh yes. Yes, my friend, I would. Most certainly I would have comforted her with my loving.'

'Why, you – you –' Alan turned away from him in incoherent rage. 'I do not understand you. A minute ago you were ready to kill me at the very thought – now you speak as if you think I should have taken her –'

Kassim gave a half-laugh that was like a snarl.

'Oh no. Not you, Alan. I would have killed you had your answer been a different one, or if I had not believed you.'

Alan stared at him, while the flames of the pyre leapt and died, and leapt up again, dancing with their own shadows on the river mud.

The man holding the horses was calling to them, and Kassim turned to the pyre and gave Mistri's father something that clinked and glittered. Payment for a dead son, thought Alan, hating him. Then he saw Kassim's face clearly for the first time, with a great gash over his forehead, clustered with dark dried blood, and forgot everything else.

'Kassim, you are badly hurt –'

'No, just a flesh wound. We had to fight to distract the attentions of a mob while Bianca and the servants got the horses away from the Madoremahal and over the river to the old dâk bungalow. Someone took a slash at me, and this is the result –

as I said, nothing. Come, to the horses. We must be ready to leave at once when she comes.' As he spoke, the horses neighed and stamped and they heard other horses coming. Rama called out suddenly and they turned to see him speaking to a man on horseback, with a led horse.

'It is Sikunder, Lord. The Begum is waiting at the next bend in the river. She is wounded, it seems, and weak, and Rhada does not think she can ride any further. Also, news has come that they are searching for riders and horses – the boat will be better.' He had hardly stopped speaking when everything burst into movement. Rama began to push the boat out, and then jumped in, taking the oars.

'Go with him, Alan – you cannot ride either because they will be looking for an Englishman. I will come with the horses – I know a way –' Kassim ran to his horse, sprang up, and was gone down the shore, followed by Sikunder and his own Syce Ayub with the two led horses.

Alan went down over the sucking mud of the shallows and climbed into the boat.

'But what of them – ?' he asked, looking back at the two beside the fire.

'They will wait until the body is consumed and then scatter the ashes on the river, and leave on foot. They mourn their dead. No one will question them.' Rama was rowing, skilfully and fast, and the current was with them. In minutes the pyre was out of sight, and they were turning for the shore again, where the river twisted inland. Alan tried to see figures on the shore, but could see nothing. The moon, perverse, had gone behind clouds, and it was very dark.

'Do not worry, Sahib – they will be there.'

They landed and Alan walked up the shore.

Seated in the shadows of an upturned boat, he found Sara, and in his relief would have taken her in his arms. But the woman with her stepped between them, and spoke words he did not understand, but her tone was as dangerous as the sudden hiss of a snake. Rama, at his elbow, said something to her, and then to Alan, his voice for the first time showing strain.

'The Sahiba is not well – she has bled very much, and is faint.'

'*Bled – ?*' said Alan stupidly. 'But how? What happened?'

'She has a bullet in her shoulder. They have bound it up, but the bullet must be removed. Any movement gives her great pain, and causes much bleeding. Oh, in the name of the gods, where is the Yuvraj? – we should take her to a Hakim –'

Alan was no longer listening. He remembered the sound of the shot, and Sara's gasp, and the way she had half turned to him – and his impatience at what he thought was a sudden loss of courage on her part.

'Oh, Sara, you were hurt, and I forced you over the wall. Sara, I am so sorry –'

She turned her head very slowly and her voice was barely above a whisper. 'If you had not forced me, we would still be prisoners – or dead. So do not be distressed.'

Her eyes were looking beyond him, and he was afraid she was fainting, until he heard the sound of galloping horses. She had heard it before he had, and so had Rama.

'Quickly, Sahib – we must carry her to the boat. Help me – these could be Hardyal's searchers.'

Alan was enraged at his own helplessness. The bullet that had lodged in Sara's shoulder must have been the one that had passed through his arm, and now he could barely summon enough strength to move his fingers. Quite impossible to help Rama support Sara. But the woman, with no word said, scooped Sara up into her arms and was striding towards the boat, and there was nothing for Alan and Rama to do but follow her. Alan did not think Sara was conscious as she was lowered into the bows. He saw the woman beckoning.

'Come, Sahib, row her downstream as far as the old bungalow, keeping to the far bank –' She broke off impatiently. 'Oh, goddess give me patience – Rama, what ails the man, can the English not manage a boat?'

'He is wounded and has, like the Begum, lost much blood.

84

You take the boat, Rhada. We will wait here and if it is the Yuvraj who comes, we will follow, swimming the ford. If it is Hardyal's men, we will lead them off somehow. Go, Rhada.'

The woman took up the oars, and pulling like a man was soon in the centre of the river, moving in and out of the fitful moonlight until she was lost to sight and even the creaking of the oars could no longer be heard.

Alan, who had sunk to the ground in a spinning weakness of nausea and pain, felt Rama's hand on his good arm.

' Sahib. Come here into the shadows. They are near.'

Near they might have been, but it seemed like an hour before the horses were actually on the river bank, and Rama, peering into the darkness, gave a deep sigh.

' The gods are with us. It is the Yuvraj and Ayub. Come, Sahib – '

Kassim wasted no time.

' Can you ride? ' he said crisply, and Alan would have died before he said no to that tone.

' Very well. Mount, and we go. Sikunder is off to see what is happening, and if necessary, he will cover our tracks. Rama, come up behind me – come on, man, what are you waiting for? '

' Heaven born, the little Begum is wounded. The bullet is still in her shoulder and we need a Hakim. Better that I go quietly to Seva Singh, and bring him – '

Kassim's silence had the quality of the silence that falls on everything before an earthquake, or a typhoon. Then he turned on Alan.

' *Why,* you thick-headed pink Englishman, did you not tell me? '

' But I did not know – ' Alan felt that his voice sounded like the bleat of a goat at the sound of the snarl of a tiger, and cursed his own wound and his weakness. Rama interrupted.

' The Major Sahib was shot also – a bullet through the arm. He has bled very much. We need a Hakim, Lord.'

Alan tried to speak with authority. ' Let us, for God's sake, go straight to the Military Hospital, Kassim, and get Sara in there. She would be safe, and Colonel Dickie is a good doctor – '

' Colonel Dickie can be blood brother to all the angels in Paradise – but can you tell me how we get her from Madore to the cantonment? Through sixteen miles of wilderness which is probably crawling with Hardyal's creatures? Sikunder says that the whole of Madore is up, and the crowds are howling with rage at the edge of the city walls, because of the fires that took hold last night. Hindu accuses Muslim and Hardyal goes round making sure that the trouble does not die down. He is using these rioting crowds for his own ends – he is determined to get Sara, and it is easier to kidnap a girl and kill her family when there is already a riot – for God's sake, Alan, think. The troops will be called in shortly – and I imagine they are still trying to find out where we have gone so that they can recall us from leave. So if we do get to the military hospital, Sara will, *if* she is accepted into a British military hospital, be left with no protection. No, Rama, go now to Seva Singh – Ayub, you go with him. Are you sure you can trust him? '

Ayub answered, ' Who knows, Maharaj? – but we will not give him time. He can come with his instruments, and afterwards – well, we can see.' Kassim waited for no more.

' Alan, get up behind me. They will need the extra horse.' Alan scrambled up, boosted from below by Rama, and before he was properly settled, Kassim kicked his animal into a swift gallop, so that Alan had to grasp him round the waist to keep his seat. Like a frightened girl, he thought, hating Kassim. Thick-headed pink Englishman – that would be wiped out one day, he vowed to himself as they rode through the cloudy night, galloping until the horse laboured beneath their double weight, and Kassim turned its head for the river, and then slid to the ground.

' Take the reins, Alan. The ford is hereabouts. I shall lead him, he'll never keep his footing with both of us on his back.'

They walked into the river, and looking over, the opposite bank seemed very far away. The horse slipped and stumbled, and then began to pick its way carefully, Kassim wading beside it, his voice a soothing murmur, up to his thighs in the swirling water.

There were lights on the shore, and Kassim said, ' Let us hope those are fisher folk, readying their nets for their night's work – because I do not think either of us would make a very good showing against our enemies at present.'

His voice was friendly and he was as he always used to be, the old Kassim who had been Alan's close friend for so long, and had so unaccountably turned into an unpleasant, sneering enemy. Alan felt that, by keeping silent, he was behaving like a sulky child. He tried to think of something to say, but the horse stumbled badly and in his weakness he had great difficulty in keeping his seat.

' Alan, can you hold him here for a little while? I want to go ahead and make sure – '

He was gone as he spoke, leaving Alan to struggle with the frightened horse, chest deep in the river, and not liking it. The few minutes that Kassim was gone were a nightmare of physical effort and fear. Then Kassim was back and, turning along parallel with the shore, he began to lead the horse again, leaving the lights behind.

At last they splashed in shallow water, and Alan felt the horse again on firm sand, and they stopped.

For a moment Kassim stood, breathing deeply, leaning against the horse, and then he mounted in front of Alan again, and took up the reins.

' They were fishers, but it seemed better for us not to appear in their midst in all our present glory. They are very poor, and Hardyal could have bribed them. Now we must move. Hold fast, Alan, while I see what speed I can get out of this poor brute.'

The horse seemed fresher for its crossing of the river – whatever the cause was, they moved at a fast gallop and within the half hour were threading between palm trees to a small marble building, its domed roof and fretted screens outlined by the setting moon.

Chapter 12

There was no light shining from the building, and Kassim cursed as he flung himself off the horse, and, taking out his dagger, went towards the steps at a stumbling run, with no effort at caution or silence.

A quiet voice spoke from the shadows. ' It is well, Kassim Khan Bahadur. They are here and we doused the lamps when we heard you coming, lest you should be the enemy.'

Goki, muffled in a shawl came up to the steps beside Kassim and called softly, ' Bianca Khanum – ' and Alan saw Bianca come out on to the verandah with a lamp. Kassim spoke first, his voice harsh with exhaustion.

' Bianca, thanks be to Allah the merciful. How is Sara? '

' Very weak, but sleeping. Is Major Reid there? '

Alan slid down from the horse, and with the last of his strength, staggered over and joined Kassim, and Bianca looked down at them both, and said suddenly, her voice desperate, ' Oh God, you are both badly hurt – what shall we do? – '

Her voice shook, and Alan held himself more upright, and straightened his shoulders.

' We are well, and you must not distress yourself, nothing is wrong – '

So saying, he pitched forward and lay at Kassim's feet, with splendid kindly unconsciousness at last taking away all thought and all pain. Kassim bent and looked at him, and then back at Bianca holding the lamp.

'As you see, we are both very well. Bianca, you are tilting the lamp and it will go out. In spite of Alan's collapse I will repeat his brave words. Do not be distressed. Alan has lost a lot of blood, and I have been very evil tempered because of – well various reasons, including a cut on the head. All we need is food and rest and the knowledge that you and Sara are safe, and we will be as strong as tigers tomorrow. Please – can I see Sara?'

He moved up the steps very carefully and slowly, as Goki came with cloths and hot water and squatted down beside Alan.

Sara lay on her side, her face very pale and her tossed hair lustreless, catching no light from the candle that Bianca lit and held so that Kassim could see her. She breathed very lightly, and her eyelashes lay on the thin hollows of her eyes, no darker than the shadows that surrounded them. Kassim bent over her for a minute, looking with drawn brows at the cloth packed round her shoulder and already staining with fresh blood. Then he straightened and said softly :

'What is that terrible smell – her wound is fresh, it cannot be suppurating – but there is a smell of something unpleasant – what is it?'

Bianca tightened her lips. 'Kassim – do not be foolish. The child has been in the temple vaults for four days, and has barely had enough water to drink and certainly no opportunity to wash. I saw that Major Reid appeared to be growing a beard – does he not smell?'

'I am used to men smelling. Not women.'

'Did you expect her to emerge from her late experiences fresh as spring water and smelling of roses?'

'No, indeed. But that is not a smell I am used to, when I am near Sara. If it is only the smell of an unwashed body, it is nothing. But if her wound is suppurating – then I want to know.'

'Well, it is not suppurating.'

She turned and walked away, taking the candle with her, and he followed, saying, 'Bianca, do not be cross with me, or if you must be cross, be only a little cross. I spoke because I can barely think, I am so relieved.'

'Relieved! How can you speak of being relieved! The city in uproar, full of evil-intentioned men searching for us – Alan Reid lying there unconscious, and Sara with a bullet in her shoulder, while we are trapped here, unable to get a doctor or anything – and you are relieved, with a great cut on your head! God, give me strength and patience.'

He saw that fear and anxiety had made her furious – fear, anxiety and guilt. He knew Bianca, and knew that she must have spent these days alone with the knowledge that her step-daughter, the beloved child of her heart, could have been safely away if it had not been for her obstinacy. So he did not answer her, and she broke into another flood of angry words.

'What are we to do? Die here, or shall we send messengers to Hardyal, telling him to come and take Sara? At least she would be safe then, he would not kill the one person who can give him Lambagh –'

'You are talking without thought, Bianca. Be quiet for a minute –' He went to the window and listened. Then he walked through to the back of the building and called softly. 'Rhada?'

'Lord?'

'You can make a fire and heat water. The Hakim is coming.'

Bianca was standing rigid, at the window, and had not heard a word he said.

'Kassim – quickly.' Her fear was so great that her body began to shake, and her husky voice was uneven. 'Kassim – they are coming. I hear horses –'

He was beside her at once, his arm about her shoulders.

'I am a fool – Bianca my dear, courage. That is Rama who comes, with Ayub, and one Seva Singh, a Hakim who is known to Rama. The bullet in Sara's shoulder must be removed –'

She sagged against him, almost fainting in her relief, and Rama and Ayub, with a man riding pillion behind him, drew rein and dismounted.

Alan still lay where he had fallen, and the Hakim checked his step beside him, but Kassim leant from the verandah to say softly, ' Up here, Seva Singh – '

The man came up the steps and into the room. He was a small man, a thin, elderly Sikh, and he had been brought in a hurry, his case of instruments in his hand, his clothes disordered. But he showed no sign of fear.

' Greetings, Nawab Sahib – where is my patient? '

' She is here. You will not speak of this – you will remain silent for your life's sake. Is that understood? '

Rama and Ayub stood watchful in the door, as the Hakim faced Kassim, looking up into his eyes for a moment. Then he said, taking a firm grip of his box of instruments, ' We waste time. I understand you,' and turned to the inner room. Kassim went in with him, and found Bianca and Goki already there, unwrapping the blood-soaked cloths from Sara's shoulder. As they uncovered the wound, she moved and opened eyes cloudy with pain, and looked round at the circle of faces, all except one known and beloved. Bianca bent over her with a soft exclamation, and Sara turned to her, her good arm raised to put round her step-mother's neck.

' Oh, *Mother* – it is so good to see you – thanks be to all the gods that you are all safe. I was so afraid for you – '

' Afraid for *us* – ' Bianca bit off her exclamation and the Hakim started his examination. Rhada came in with hot water, and Kassim, after a quick look at the wound, spoke to Ayub, who went out and brought in a silver flask from Kassim's saddle bag.

' Seva Singh – you have opium? '

The Hakim looked up at him, his lips drawn tight, and shook his head.

' Nay. I was not given time. I wish I had, for this bullet is lodged very deep.'

Kassim moved forward until he could stand beside Sara, opposite the Hakim.

' Well, moon of delight – how is it with you? '

Sara tried to answer his bantering voice as lightly, but her voice trembled as she spoke.

' It is well with me, oh Lord of ten thousand horsemen. But Kassim – it pains me very much, and I am afraid – '

' Sarajan, do not be afraid. Listen, you are going to drink so much brandy that you will feel nothing – and I will hold your hands, and you will be looking at me, and it will be all over before you know – ' His voice broke suddenly and his eyebrows drew together in a tight black bar. He stared down at Sara's face, and for a moment his expression was like a devil's mask.

Sara's eyes widened with fear, and she asked, ' Kassim – what is it? ' and then he was smiling apologetically, saying, ' Forgive me – my head pained me. So – now we drink together, sip for sip, like lovers at a feast – see, Princess of love and beauty, I toast your eyes – '

He took a long swallow and then put the flask to her mouth, holding her up so that she could drink and as she choked on the fiery liquid, he laid her back on her pillows, took another drink himself, and kissing the edge of the flask, put it to her lips again, saying, ' See – thus lovers drink – ' and then he gestured with his head at Seva Singh to begin.

The flask clattered against Sara's teeth, and the brandy ran down her chin as she bit on her own lip. Then the scream she was trying to hold back, rang through the room, and she fell into black darkness shot through with flashes of scarlet agony, until at last she reached perfect unconsciousness and was out of reach of what they were doing to her. Bianca stood like a rock, her hands holding the cloths, and Goki held the basin of reddening water and Kassim held the quiet body, and looked down at the white face with the scarred cheek, and called on death for Hardyal in his mind. He glanced once at Bianca and saw on her face the same look that he knew was on his own face – undying hatred and determination. Then, as Sara moved, and groaned under the Hakim's probing instruments, he murmured soothingly and turned all his attention to watching the Hakim.

He heard Bianca's breath drawn in great gasps as the probes grated on something. With a muttered ' Thanks be to Allah ' he saw the pincers go in, and come out, grasping a bit of metal.

92

' It is good,' said Seva Singh quietly. ' The bullet is complete and I can find no fragments of bone. The lady is young and will heal.'

His hands were quick, and skilful, and Sara's wound was closed and stitched and bound with clean cloth, and then Kassim laid her flat on the bed. Looking at her still, deathly pale face, darkly shadowed round the lips and eyes, he wondered if the treatment had not done more damage than the wound. Bianca spoke for the first time.

' Hakim – she has a cheek wound – is all well with it? '

The man bent close above the ugly puckered scar, still purple and slightly suppurating. He sniffed, and then raised his head, an expression of sorrow on his face.

' It is healing. It is clean. But what a terrible scar it will leave. The lady will bear that mark all her days – I can do nothing to help that.' He turned to Kassim, and saw his expression.

' Nawab Sahib. She is already recovering. Rest your mind. Now sit, and let me see that wound on your head.'

Kassim sat, and felt the gentle, light fingers grow hard and painful, so that his head throbbed and a trickle of blood ran down his cheek. Seva Singh cleaned the wound, saying, ' You are fortunate – you too will be scarred for the rest of your life. But another hair's breadth down and you would have lost the sight of that eye. Now, let me see the Sahib – ' He got up and walked out, and Kassim and Bianca looked at each other over Sara's bed.

' May Allah forgive us – ' said Kassim. ' I had forgotten " The Sahib " – and yet there is no doubt that Sara would be married to Hardyal and gone from us if it had not been for Alan's courage. If only – '

He did not finish what he was saying, but went out, leaving Bianca and Goki clearing up the disorder of the room, removing all trace of what had taken place there.

Bianca, as she worked, her long delicate fingers red with Sara's blood, thought how hard and desperate Kassim's face had looked, and remembered the laughing boy she had known ten years before. She remembered other things too, and did not know that her face also bore the hard cruel grimace that Kassim's face had worn – the face of a killer.

Chapter 13

Alan was conscious, but quiet as the Hakim cleaned his wound and bound it up.

Kassim came down the steps and found that Alan was lying, propped against the wall, and the Hakim was just finishing the bandaging. In the shadows beyond the circle of light thrown by a small lantern, Rama stood with Ayub, and Kassim walked over to them.

' He asks no questions, and seems to know all of us.'

' Yea, Lord. But he swears he is a man of healing and belongs to no faction.'

' That is as maybe.' Ayub's voice was a growl.

' The risk is too great. Let me take him home, Lord. I will be sure that he returns safely whence he came, and says nothing to anyone. This place is unknown, or Hardyal's men would have been here by now. I think it better that the Hakim goes safely home – to silence.'

While Kassim was listening to Ayub, he saw Rama glance over to the light, and turned his own eyes that way. The Hakim had finished, and was standing facing them, his box of instruments in his hands, his face still and watchful. Alan too had raised his head from the wall, and called out to Kassim.

' Kassim, is Sara all right? '

Kassim went over to him.

' Yes, she is not conscious, but the bullet is out, and the Hakim says that there is no sign of inflammation.'

' Thank God for that. But we will not be able to move on for some days, will we? '

Something about Kassim's still silence got through to him. He stopped speaking, cursing himself, and Kassim gave an imperceptible shrug.

' No. We will have to stay here for at least three days before we go back to the Madoremahal.'

Alan said nothing. The five men were all quiet, the two outside the light holding the horses, and the three grouped together in the circle of light. A bat, blinded by the light, swooped low over their heads, and a moth was blundering against the lamp glass, making a soft sound like whispering voices.

The Hakim spoke at last.

' I go, Nawab Sahib? '

' Yes, Hakimji. You go.'

Ayub pulled his horse forward, and the Hakim said, on a higher note, ' Nay – there is no need for me to ride again, as if chased by devils, as I was brought here. I will go on foot to the ferry and cross there, and make my own way home. I am well known in the fishing village. If I do not return home, they will come to question the fishermen – and the village is very close to this place. It is better that I go home as I am used to going, on my feet. It is better for all – horses are noticed in my street.'

He waited a moment, watching Kassim's face, and then said, ' I am needed in the city. There are many wounded.' He looked then straight into Kassim's eyes. ' I go, Lord? '

' Why have you asked no questions, Hakim? '

' Because I know all that is necessary.'

' How? '

' I am a man of Jindbagh. I was trained by the white Hakim, him they called Reiss. I remember Lambagh well. My work is here in Madore, but I will come back to the hills soon. I grow old. I would like to die in my own place.'

Ayub's horse tossed its head, its harness jingling, the moth whispered round the lamp, and those two sounds seemed very loud in the silence. Kassim saw Rama and Ayub turn away, heir horses pulled after them, and he nodded.

' Very well, Hakimji. Go your own way.'

The Hakim sighed deeply, touched his forehead and said, My life for yours, Lord – ' and was gone on the words, his feet making no sound. Alan watching, knew that he had just seen a man reprieved from death. The idea of the Hakim, who had just bound up his wound with skilful fingers, being murdered to ensure his silence and their safety was merely a part of all the horrifying things that seemed to have started happening ever since the day he had entered the Madoremahal. He was weak from loss of blood, and dazed and tired, and could feel nothing very much. Tides of sleep were beginning to wash over him. Kassim took his good arm and helped him up the steps on to the verandah and put him in a long chair. When he brought out a blanket and a pillow he found Alan already asleep, and he did not move as Kassim put the pillow under his head and the blanket over him. Kassim left him lying there and went inside, his head full of plans and arrangements, his wound throbbing.

Bianca and Goki were waiting for him, and they made him sit, and Goki brought them both glasses of hot milk laced with brandy, and then padded off to sit with Sara.

' Sara needs to stay, resting, for four days – at least,' said Bianca. ' But I suppose that is out of the question.' Kassim nodded. ' Yes. We can stay tomorrow, I think. But then we must go – and we must go without returning to Madore, and moving as fast as possible – do you think Sara can do it? '

Bianca shrugged. ' For her life, she must. And Major Reid? '

' He comes with us – more or less. He has nearly three months' leave left. If he goes back now, Hardyal's men will get him. He will be well enough to ride tomorrow – in fact, as I think of it, it would be best if he went off early in the morning, taking three men with him, and meeting us at Favidkote. For one thing, if there is a pursuit it might divert them to have another party to follow.'

' Is it fair to get him entangled in this affair? '

' Perfectly fair. For one thing, he is my friend. For another, the

poor man imagines himself in love with Sara – and mo
important of all, if we have him with us, he is a danger. The
are looking for an Englishman. He must, for our sakes and h
own, be got safely away.'

' You do not sound as if you are his friend – '

' Oh, but I am – alas. I am very fond of him. Otherwise
would have killed him. He is utterly trustworthy, very brave an
a complete fool. All these things combine to make him a grea
danger in an enterprise like ours.'

' Kassim! How can you speak so of your friend, who save
Sara? – '

' Do not forget it was his lack of control that allowed her t
fall into danger to start with. He should never have let her g
near the river – and should have brought her back at once
Oh, do not let us speak of him any longer. He goes off in th
morning. We move by night. Are you sure you can do th
journey? '

Bianca was looking out into the dark garden, sitting as he ha
so often seen her, slender hands holding her cup, her face i
profile as delicate and lovely as a cameo.

' I can do it, of course. But – '

For a moment the lovely mouth trembled and broke into
grimace of sorrow.

' How far do I come? '

' What do you mean, Bianca? '

' You *know* what I mean,' she replied, and her straight loo
silenced him for a while.

' Bianca – this separation has always been of your own wish
You come as far as you wish to come. You know that. Do yo
still feel horror at the thought of going back? '

' No. No, I do not.'

' Then, what are you talking about? Surely you know the so
of welcome that you will have.'

' Do I? It has been ten years, Kassim. But never mind tha
We will see. There are other things to think about. There i
food for the journey. Dry rations, I mean. There are twelv

98

nen, not counting you and Rama and Ayub, and four women – '

' *Four?* '

' Rhada comes too. It would not be safe for her to go back.
he is very worried about Muna.'

' Muna will be all right. She is too well known and too popular
or anyone to harm her. Strange – how she pays her debts, that
ne ! '

' Goki is very proud.'

' She has a right to be. Saving Muna's life was the best thing
he ever did in a long life of service to my house. But listen –
ever mind Muna now. We will talk of her when we reach
afety. There are other things, as you said.'

They continued to speak quietly of arrangements and organi-
ations for the next day, sipping their drinks, gradually falling
lent. Presently Bianca saw that Kassim at last had relaxed and
allen asleep. Getting up, she covered him with a blanket and sat
eside him, while the last of the dark hours passed and the sky
egan to streak with reds and yellows of dawn. When the first
arrots flew screaming from the trees, he woke to find her sitting
here, and was distressed to think that she had not slept, but she
hook her head at his protests, and said, ' I had a great deal to
hink about. Now I will go and get tea, and perhaps you will
ouse Major Reid, and bring him in. Goki says Sara is sleeping
ow, and very deeply, so all is well – '

Chapter 14

Alan, wakened, was a new man. His first demand was for a razor and he went off to the river bank with towel and soap and came back shaved and clean and cheerful.

Bianca had not yet seen him. When he went into the house she was waiting for him, and going forward took his hand in both hers and said, 'I cannot thank you, Major Reid, but you will understand how I feel. You are part of my family now, and always will be.'

Alan had a reply on his lips, but his words left him when he saw how exhausted and drained her face looked, and how thin she had become, and he bent and kissed the hands that held his and turned away, too moved to speak.

Kassim, lounging in the window, said, 'Now here is an improvement! No beard, and no words! You were as full of both yesterday as a temple fakir, and smelt as bad –' He made room for Alan on the window seat beside him, and pulled out his cigar case and went on talking until he saw Alan was pulling on his cigar and was in command of himself again. Then he leaned forward.

'Alan – we do thank you – indeed, we owe you a great debt which we can never repay. Without you, that girl sleeping in that room would either be dead, or worse, married to Hardyal – and shortly after that there would have been terrible uprisings in the hill States.' He paused, and looked carefully at Alan.

'We are not yet able to stop and rest in safety. Sara cannot be moved today – but you are well, and feeling strong again?'

Alan nodded, waiting.

'Good. Now, listen. You go off, after you have had your morning tea, with three men and Rhada, the girl who brought Sara in last night. You will ride by the Shikri road to Faridkote, two days and two nights. When you get there, wait – we leave tonight, and should meet you on the second night after you reach Faridkote. Ayub Khan will be one of the men with you, he will show you where to wait, and I do not think you will have any trouble, but if you do, it will be because you are keeping danger from us. Will you help us again, Alan? You understand all that it means?'

Alan understood well enough that he was to be a decoy, and stood an excellent chance of being captured on the road. For a second, a sort of astonishment held him silent. What was he doing, caught in this monstrous web of plots and intrigues with a family he had never heard of until a few days before – except for his friend Kassim? And Kassim had been far from friendly yesterday. Yet here he was, almost begging Alan to help him.

'You will wear some of my clothes, of course, and Rhada will be dressed in Sara's robes.' Sara! That of course was what he would be doing – helping Sara to safety.

Alan smiled, and said, 'Of course I understand. I'll try and act my part well – the arrogance and general rudery will be difficult and I will have to slouch a bit more than I care to –'

Bianca heard them laughing when she came in with glasses of tea, and realised with sudden astonishment that they were two very young men – in their early thirties.

Why, I too, she thought wonderingly, I am only twenty-six – a young woman! She put the thought away, and took the tea over to the two men sitting in the window, and sat watching them drink it, unable to swallow her own.

Alan drank quickly, and was standing, putting on Kassim's high-collared coat and complaining of the fit.

'Terribly tight, my dear fellow – you must be as thin as a

girl. I dare not flex my muscles, you can see – '

Kassim, conscious of his own wide shoulders and extra height smiled. ' It is a difference of build, rather than size – you have the shoulders and chest of one of your English bulls. I, on the other hand, have the strength and muscle of the tiger – '

The sudden arrival of Rhada, wearing Sara's creamy white robes, interrupted their bickering. Kassim looked at her and under his gaze she turned slowly and pulled her head cloth more closely over her face.

' Yes. Well, at a distance, Rhada, I suppose one who did no know the Begum might mistake you. Alan, you should no complain about my coat. See how Sara's bodice cramps Rhada's magnificent opulence – '

Alan expected the girl to be embarrassed by so much male scrutiny, but she laughed at Kassim and said, ' Yea, Lord, le us hope it is only at a distance that they see me – for the marigold can never hope to masquerade as the jasmine.'

Kassim smiled at her with a warmth and friendship that Alan had not seen on his face since the troubles had begun. ' Well said, Rhada. But be sure of one thing, we will all win to safety and when we do, the marigold will bloom in splendour and be treated as a queen for the rest of her life.'

Rhada stooped with pliant grace to touch his feet, and then stepped back, and stood waiting. Kassim turned to answer a question from Rama.

' No – they will ride together – they will expect Sara to be riding behind the Major Sahib, especially if they know she had been wounded.'

' Do they know? ' asked Alan.

' Only if Seva Singh is a traitor. But in any case, they know about the branding. When was *that* done, Alan? '

' Just after I got to the front of the crowd. I had no idea what they were about to do or I would have moved faster – i happened literally before I rushed them.'

It was as if he was speaking of something that had happened to someone else, it all seemed so long ago.

' I never actually saw the brand,' he said slowly. ' Not properly. It was very dark in the vaults. She was so brave – she made no complaint – ' He broke off, shocked at the thought of the pain Sara had silently endured, and recalled how he had flinched away from applying the green ointment to that horrible area of burned flesh that had smelt like grilled meat. Kassim broke into his unhappy thoughts.

' Alan, who did the branding? '

' The chief priest. I killed him, but not in time. But it was Hardyal who ordered it to be done. Why did he brand her? Surely it is not one of your marriage customs, is it? '

Kassim gave him a long cool stare.

' No, my dear Alan, it is not. But I dare say it pleased Hardyal to set his mark on her. I have heard that centuries ago in the south this was sometimes done – he merely revived an old custom.' His voice sounded like the snarl of the tiger he had likened himself to in jest.

Alan stood up abruptly.

' May I see the Begum before I go? I will not waken her.'

Bianca said that of course he could. Kassim did not move from his lounging position in the window, but Alan was certain that he would have stopped him going to see Sara if he could have done. He followed Bianca, and stood beside the bed, looking at Sara sleeping, and his shock showed on his face. The scar lay on the soft skin of her cheek like a scarlet and purple star. Her eyelashes, long and tangled, hid the shadows under her eyes, but all the bones of her face were showing. She looked terribly frail, and against the white pillows her face was shadowed and sallow. All her beauty had left her, thought Alan – my poor girl, all your girlhood and your bloom gone. Bianca saw his face and drew him quietly from the room.

' It is hard to leave someone you love, I know,' she said. ' But it will not be long before we will all meet at Faridkote, and then Sara will be awake and able to talk to you.' She felt Kassim looking at her, and met his gaze defiantly – and found that he was no longer looking at her, in fact. He was staring hard at Alan.

The silence stretched, and Kassim broke it by standing up, and saying, 'Well, Alan, I think if you are ready, you should go. Wait – you must of course have my turban.' He snatched up a long length of yellow muslin, and Alan sat while Kassim folded it round his head. 'There, now you look like a hill prince – more or less. In the name of Allah, keep that on – Rhada will tie it for you. Your hair is too fair, which is a nuisance – Rhada, if you have an opportunity, dye his hair, will you? Alan, your entourage awaits you – Rhada makes a most personable companion for a young man, but no one could mistake her curvaceous person for Sara's slim body.' Alan found Kassim's sardonic gaze disturbing – it was to him as if Kassim knew more about him than he knew of himself. He bowed stiffly to Bianca and was deeply touched when she put her arms round his neck and kissed him, and then she turned quickly away and went into Sara's room. Kassim, followed by Alan, went out to the horses. Kassim looked at the horses and shook his head.

'Your mare is not up to carrying both of you – there isn't an animal here that is. Oh rose of love and beauty ' – he had turned to Rhada, speaking in the vernacular – ' oh princess of delights – I doubt if any one horse could carry both thy richness and the Major Sahib as well. So we will trust that you will not be followed too closely.'

Rhada mounted, and pulled her veil over her face. Alan, mounting Bedami, remembered suddenly his last ride with Sara, seeing the white robes, so white that once again they caught reflections from the river and the trees. But other than the robes there was nothing here to stir his memories. This girl Rhada was most certainly not going to be mistaken for Sara, even at a great distance. But at least, if questioned, people would say that a man and a girl and three of a bodyguard had passed, and while this was being investigated, Sara and her party might get further on their journey.

Kassim came and stood by him.

'God speed, my friend. Take no risks. I look forward to our shooting trip – even if delayed.' Alan took the hand held out to

him and gripped it, looking down into the smiling friendly face
he knew so well – his friend and comrade, Kassim. Then he
turned his horse and rode off, thinking to himself that Kassim
had as many faces as a prism, and that he could not understand
him at all.

Chapter 15

Kassim watched until the dust cloud of their going was small in the distance and then went back to Bianca.

' Well, dearest aunt, that is one fence we have built, however rickety. Now let us look to the others.' He called Rama, and asked about horses.

' They are here, Lord, all of them safe. Back from the house on the river bank. Sakhi Mohammed is also here, and Sikunder Khan and four of his men. They guard the approaches. I myself and Sita Ram are with the horses, and Sikunder's son is in that mango tree on the ridge; he will give us warning if any come that way.'

Kassim nodded, satisfied, and stood for a minute longer looking out at the day, already beginning to breathe of heat to come.

' Rama, did you see the branding? '

' Yea, Lord. I was in the crowd.'

' Was it as the Sahib said – did Hardyal order it? '

' It was as the Sahib said. Hardyal watched till the iron was hot, and said something to the priest and then the priest took the branding iron and put it to the Begum's face – the Sahib shot and killed him at once.'

Kassim's face was so terrible in its controlled rage that Rama stopped speaking.

' What did they use? What was the brand? '

Rama, glancing at his face, compressed his lips, took a deep breath, and said, almost whispering :

'They branded the Begum Sahiba with the brand they use on their horses. It is a small star – but at least the man who did it is dead, and died in agony. The Sahib shot him in the stomach.'

'And Hardyal still lives. Is there any more damage his family can do to ours? Does Allah sleep?'

Rama made no reply, watching Kassim, and then when he judged his presence forgotten, he went away, down to the river bank where the horses were tethered, stamping and switching their tails under the trees.

Kassim went into the house and found Bianca.

'Does Sara still sleep?' Bianca nodded, and he asked to go in and see her.

He had his first full sight of Sara's face in the daylight, and Bianca heard his indrawn breath as he looked. She could not see his face, for her own eyes were full of tears. Her beautiful little Sara, the child of her heart, her gentle, loving child – outside the room, when she could speak, she said, 'It will fade, that scar – but what has happened within her? That is what worries me. She has been frightened and hurt badly – in body. If only her mind is unwounded. They drugged her too, you know – Alan told me. She did not feel the branding, because they drugged her. Supposing –' His deep voice interrupted her.

'Bianca. They drugged her to keep her quiet. You were drugged in a different way –' He stopped as she shuddered and turned away, then he put his hands on her shoulders and made her look at him.

'You told me you were better – do the devils still ride in your dreams?'

'No – no. But I still fear –'

'Fear what? Five years ago I could not have held you thus. Three years ago you still could not stand to be assisted into your saddle by a man, and Goki said you still screamed in your sleep. And now?'

'Until this trouble started, I had begun to sleep in peace – and your touch is the touch of my dear and beloved friend.'

' And you kissed Alan – '

' Why, yes – so I did – I had forgotten – '

' You are well, cured. Do not make yourself ill again by imagining vain things about Sara. She will recover and be as she always was – her hurts were, thanks be to Allah, all physical. Come – drink a little wine with me, and we will plan our journey – for as soon as she wakes, I think we should go, without waiting for the night – I have a feeling – '

Sitting beside him in the window seat, she found all his plans good. As he heard her agreeing so readily, Kassim thought for a bitter second, ' Oh you fool, Bianca – had you listened thus to me when I first warned you, we would not be in such danger now, and you and Sara would be safely in Lambagh.' He kept his thoughts to himself; it seemed she had suffered enough for her recalcitrance. So they sat, peaceably planning – Bianca would ride her own horse, Sara would ride with Sakhi Mohammed, and he himself would come some distance behind with Rama and two of the other men. Sikunder Khan would go first, with Goki pillion with him.

' You will be a family party – a Begum from Nucklao with her daughter and servants. They are not looking for anything like that, as far as I know. We will have to ride hard, Bianca – you should start making ready now.'

She left him, her long silken skirts trailing behind her, and he watched her, wondering to himself what she had become, and how she would manage to live through the difficult days ahead. He recalled the lovely, laughing girl he had first met, only ten years ago, and could see no resemblance in this beautiful controlled yet self-willed woman to that happy girl. He turned away from his memories, and began again to check his plans for their journey, working stage by stage of each day's travel in his mind. He could not bear to think of the pain that was going to be inflicted on Sara with her wounded shoulder being jerked by every step the horses took – but there was no other way. If only they had a palanquin! He groaned when he remembered the many palanquins and dandies standing gathering dust in the store room of the Madoremahal – just one of those would make all the difference. Possibly, he thought with sudden horror, all the difference between life and death for Sara.

He stared at the shadows growing smaller on the grass. In a moment he would have to waken Sara. The verandah seats against the railing were already in full sun, and the heat was growing.

He heard a parrot scream from the mango tree on the ridge, and saw Sakhi Mohammed and Sikunder go forward, walking casually in single file, as villagers walk when they go to look at their fields. He called softly to Bianca, 'Stay within – someone comes – ' and himself dropped below the window ledge, and waited, his rifle ready.

Presently he heard Sakhi Mohammed's voice calling to him, and he stood up to see the two men, with a woman standing between them.

There was no mistaking who the woman was. It was Muna, the temple dancer, and one of the most famous harlots in the north. He recalled her as he had first seen her, a slender child playing about the small palace in Lambagh, Sara's constant companion and beloved adopted sister, the child that Goki had rescued from beside her dying mother during the terrible killings of 1857 – the year of the Mutiny. Now she was rich and famous and very popular. Still in her early youth, she showed the marks of her profession in her face, the knowledgeable eyes, the curved painted mouth, and the trained voluptuous walk and stance. But none of that was to be despised. This was a very powerful lady. Also, she was devoted to the House of Lambagh, and had already helped Sara – once when she became a temple dancer in Sara's place, and now again in the difficult rescue from the temple.

She greeted Kassim with a dancer's deep sweeping obeisance and said, 'Lord, I bring news.'

'You are as welcome as water in the desert, Munabhen. Speak.'

'The city is like a wasps' nest torn down from a wall. They

have burned the street of the Harlots to the ground. The men of Hardyal are still searching the temple and all the streets round it.

' And the Madoremahal? '

' All is quiet there, Lord. I saw the wife of the dâk carrier last night. It is known to all that the house is empty. The woman did not think that anyone had been near the house for a week – not since the horses were taken out.'

' What do they think has happened to us? '

' They know the little Begum was captured – most of them saw her branded. Hardyal is not beloved. There are many tales about the rest of you – some say that you are all dead – others that you yourself are dead, and the others escaped to the hills with the Sahib.' She stopped speaking when she saw he was no longer listening to her but was deep in thought.

It was Sakhi Mohammed who asked, ' Why do they think the Yuvraj is dead? '

' It was the pyre on the river bank. Mistri's parents had gone, having scattered the ashes – but the Yuvraj had left his blood-stained turban there, and there were traces of incense and sandalwood – they think you burned his body because there was no time for a Muslim burial. They do not, therefore, search for the Yuvraj – only for the Sahib and the Begums – both of them.

Kassim stared at them all without seeing them. His thoughts were with the deserted Madoremahal and the palanquins stored there – just one of those palanquins for Sara. It would slow their journey of course, but that could not be helped.

He beckoned to Sakhi Mohammed, and told Muna to go into the house and see Goki. Then he took Sakhi by the arm.

' Listen, Sakhi – how think you? The Madoremahal is deserted. The little Begum is injured and weak and riding will be very hard for her – if not impossible. If we four – Rama, you, myself and Sita Ram, make our way to the Mahal and bring back a palanquin – '

Sakhi Mohammed nodded. ' Yea, Lord – that is a good plan. But it is not necessary for you to come. Three of us can bring the palanquin – there are old ones there for two carriers – you should be here in case of trouble – '

But Kassim was not listening to him.

' That leaves the boy, and your four men to guard the ladies. It will have to do. Tell Rama to bring the horses closer to the house, and put the men with them. If any of Hardyal's men come, your men must take the Begum Sarajan and ride for Faridkote and through to the hills, stopping for nothing. The Begum Bianca will take one horse and ride towards Multalla, dressed in her daughter's clothes.' Swiftly he outlined his plan, and Sakhi Mohammed made no more argument, seeing it was useless.

' We will go down the river by boat, to the old landing stage. Then Rama can bring the boat back and we three will carry the palanquin – one in front and two behind. Go – tell Rama and Sita Ram, and I will tell the Begum Bianca.'

Bianca, who had found Sara burning with fever, made no demur when he told her of his plan.

She watched them leave. Muna went with them.

' I can go ahead into the house, Lord, and warn you – or better, I can watch the road ! '

Kassim agreed. Bianca thought that he was so determined on his mission that nothing really got through to him. His mind was set like a compass-needle, and indeed his idea was no longer only a possibility – it was a necessity. Now it was obvious that without a palanquin it would be impossible to move Sara. She was very feverish, and her shoulder wound looked angry and inflamed. All the same, Bianca was amazed at how lightly Kassim had left them. Four armed men, however competent, would not be enough if Hardyal attacked in force.

Goki, sitting beside Sara with a palm leaf fan to keep off the insistent flies, tried to put her mind at rest.

' Hardyal cannot attack in force, from what I hear from Muna. He is in trouble. He has caused so much damage in the city with his paid trouble-makers that everyone is against him. The fire that burned the street of Harlots to the ground spread to the Goldsmiths' market and the street of the Silk Merchants.

The landlords are very angry, also the bankers and the Muslim leaders, because he has tried to implicate them. Do not worry about Hardyal for the moment, Bianca – rest, all will be well.'

Bianca thought of all the many times in her life when Goki's voice had soothed her fears. But now, with Sara tossing in fever, and their lives (no doubt about it) in desperate danger, she found Goki's suggestion that she should rest far from calming. She busied herself packing the stores into *kiltas,* the leather covered baskets, cone-shaped, that the hill men carried on their backs. Then, hot and tired, she went into the bathroom and splashed her face with cold water. Drying her face, she stared at herself in the mirror – haggard and hollow-eyed with fatigue, and with her hair half down, she suddenly took all her hair down, and then began to unbutton the tight bodice of her full-skirted, many petticoated dress. Free of all constricting clothes, her breasts were as white and fresh as a girl's – at least her body had not changed. She need have no fears of looking old and repulsive if – her mind turned away from a half-formed thought. She went through to the room where the bags and bundles were stacked and began to search through them. Then, carrying an assortment of clothing, she went back to the bathroom and began to bathe.

Half an hour later, bathed and refreshed, she went quietly into Sara's room, and Goki looked at her as she came in, and stood up, saying, ' Now this is indeed a good and sensible thing to do – and how beautiful you look, my Bianca. You give pleasure to the eyes. So you looked, when you were a girl.' Bianca had dressed herself in the robes that all the hill women of Lambagh wore. Cream, natural light wool, light as silk. Her great shadowed blue eyes were half veiled in the white folds of a muslin head cloth, her long hair so widely striped with silver, hung in a thick plait to her waist. She smiled at Goki's words, but her eyes, as usual, were expressionless. Goki sighed and turned back to Sara, who had fallen into a deep sleep, her face no longer flushed, but very pale.

' Goki – go eat and rest. I will stay with Sara, and when you have eaten, bring me some tea.'

Goki crept out, leaving step-mother and daughter together. Outside, the sun was high, and the heat was growing. Bianca could see a turn of the river, flowing sluggishly between green banks. No sign of movement, human or animal, showed anywhere. Even the parrots and the crows were quiet, deep in the green shade of the mango trees. A movement from Sara drew her attention back to the bed. The girl was awake, and staring at her. Bianca was afraid that Sara would not recognise her, dressed as she was, but, as she put out a reassuring hand, Sara said, ' Mother – how beautiful you look – how beautiful! Why did you never dress like this before – you used to though, I can remember, in Lambagh – you never wore anything else – why not here? '

While Bianca was trying to think of an answer, Sara nodded her head.

' How stupid I am – of course I know why. You wanted no memories of Lambagh – were you very unhappy there? ' Her voice, weakened to a thread, was so full of tenderness that Bianca could have wept.

' No – I was very happy in Lambagh.'

Sara stared at her. ' But then, why did we come and live in Madore for so long – did you hate my father? Oh mother, was he so terrible, was he a monster? Was that why you screamed so often in your sleep, and used to get up and walk about in your room? Please tell me – ' Her eyes were full of pity, and of fear. The man she spoke of was her own father.

Bianca, in the quiet room, alone with Sara, caught in some strange feeling of being in a limbo in time, found it suddenly easy to tell the truth.

' No – your father is a wonderful man. He is kind, gentle, honest and very brave.'

' Then you did not love him? '

' I loved him with all my heart. I still do. You know, I was only a year older than you are now when I left him,' said Bianca, and her memory pictured for her those days in Lambagh when she was first married, the happy days of her young loving, and her control broke, and putting her head down on the pillow beside Sara's head, she wept.

Goki, coming in with Bianca's glass of tea, found them both in tears.

'What, then, is this? A cure for fears and fevers? Come, Sahiba, this is not good for the child – '

But when Bianca had risen, and was drying her eyes, Goki, smoothing back Sara's hair and straightening her bed, was delighted to find her soaked and sweating. The fever had broken. They washed her, and put her in clean robes, and Sara announced that she felt hungry, and also demanded a comb, and looked more like herself than Bianca had seen her look since her capture. But Sara did not ask for a mirror, and when she sat up to have her hair combed, she rested one hand on her cheek, screening her cheek from their eyes. Bianca's heart ached for her, but she said nothing, for there was nothing to say then. Later she would find ways of comforting Sara, and explaining that one scar did not make her ugly. But it seemed better to be silent now.

Presently Sara was drinking broth brought by Goki.

'Where did you conjure *that* from?' asked Bianca. 'I did not know that we had any chicken.'

'Muna brought it when she came – and fresh bread and vegetables too.'

'Muna! Oh, I want to see her!'

'You will – she comes back very soon. She has gone with Kassim to try and get a palanquin for you.' Sara was bright-eyed with pleasure.

'It will be wonderful to speak to Muna after so long. You know, it was her voice calling to me from the street that made me jump – otherwise I would still be sitting on top of that wall, it was so high. And then, she saved me in the house, when a drunk man tried to take me. She tore her bodice open and showed him her breasts, and laughed at him and he left me and ran after her. He was a horrible man, old, and his breath smelled. Muna's breasts – just the ends of them – were painted with gold paint, like the statue of the goddess in the temple. She is very beautiful. Is it not strange, Mother, that this is the second time Munabhen has saved me? If she had not given herself to the temple to serve the goddess, so that my father could keep me, I might now be in her place, with my breasts painted gold on the ends, having to make love with horrible old men – ugh – I owe Munabhen so much that I can never repay.'

'You are right. But drink your broth, child – for as you are now, you have nothing to put gold paint on – you are like a handful of bones.'

Goki spoke calmly, but Bianca could think of nothing to say at all. Her carefully guarded Sara! She looked at her, sitting propped up in bed, drinking broth. She looked like a child, a child who had been hurt, yet here she was, talking about drunken men and Muna's gold-tipped breasts – and her eyes were as clear and steady as they had always been, above that dreadful scar. She bent forward and kissed her step-daughter, and Sara smiled at her with love.

Chapter 16

The crossing of the river was without event. Kassim began, indeed, to feel that he was dreaming. Nothing stirred on the bank, no one intercepted them, as they dodged through the bushes and trees until they reached the road.

The road itself was empty. At first they edged their way along, from tree to tree, waiting and listening. Nothing else moved, except the birds, going about their daily business, parrots and crows, and rustling among the lower branches the busy seven sisters, grey-brown birds that always moved in groups of seven. Otherwise there was nothing.

They walked on to the shade-barred road and went boldly towards the city, seeing and hearing nothing but the birds. The red walls of the Madoremahal were there ahead – no one challenged them as they came up to the closed gates. Leaving Muna at the side of the road to give them warning if anyone came, Kassim and the others went down the side wall to the back of the garden, between the wall and the thorn hedge, to where there was a small gate. It was closed, but not locked. Kassim pushed it open, and they ran in, and lay panting behind the bushes of bougainvillaea and oleander, peering at the Madoremahal that sprawled in front of them, the shutters closed, silent in the sun. Slowly they worked their way round through the empty stables to the godown where the palanquins were stored. The door was shut and bolted, the lock in place.

' Wait, Lord – I will open it.' Rama moved silently over to the door, and taking the key from his shirt pocket, undid the lock. To do this, he had to break cover, completely, but no one came, no shots were fired. The garden was as quiet and peaceful under the hot sun as if nothing had ever happened there. Rama swung the door open, and the other three ran over and into the dusty darkness of the great high ceilinged godown.

Kassim knew exactly what he wanted – he passed the heavily carved and gilded palanquins and went to the back of the room where the dandies were stored. He found what he was looking for almost at once, a light travelling palanquin, made to be carried by only two men. It was made of woven cane, and was dusty and hung with cobwebs, but otherwise appeared to be in perfect condition. Rama took his shirt off, and dusted the palanquin quickly, and when it was clean, Rama and Sita Ram lifted it and carried it through the shadows to the door.

It was then that they heard a sound that made them all stand frozen and still, barely breathing – a hand was fumbling at the door outside. Kassim took out his dagger and saw Sakhi Mohammed do the same. The others drew back, and Sakhi Mohammed, with Kassim behind him, stood to one side of the door as it slowly opened a crack and a figure slipped through.

Kassim stopped Sakhi's downward stab in mid-air.

It was Muna who stood there, gasping and peering through the dust-laden shadows at them.

' Quickly – there is a band of men coming from Madore – it is many men, and they are moving fast. Now they are about ten minutes from us.' She looked at the palanquin as Sakhi Mohammed and Sita Ram raised it, and Rama pulled the door open. She stopped them and said, ' Lord – do you and Rama go into the fields and meet us round the curve in the road. I will ride in the palanquin and Sakhi Mohammed and Sita Ram are my servants, carrying me to Meerut, after my house was burned. Those men out there will not stop me. They know me. But you, Lord, they would stop – and Rama, they will remember him as the Begum Sahiba's servant. Go quickly – I will lock the door.'

She snatched the key from Rama and locked the godown door

as Rama and Kassim ran out of the garden. Then she seated herself in the palanquin and, with one man latching the gate behind her, she was carried out into the road.

The men coming from Madore were almost at the main gate, and the palanquin was in full view. There was a shouting from the mob, and then from the rabble one man rode out.

'Stop!' His voice held authority, and Muna's heart sank, but she spoke quickly.

'Do as he says.'

Her bearers stopped and lowered the palanquin to the ground. The rider stopped beside it, and with his sword, pushed aside the light curtain that hung before Muna, and looked down at her.

As they had run through the garden, she had snatched a scarlet hibiscus – with the flower arranged in her shining hair, she leaned indolently back in the palanquin, arms folded behind her head, full bosom outthrust, and looked back at the man on the horse, with bold sparkling eyes that did not waver before his stare.

'Who are you? Where do you go?'

His voice was unfriendly and the sword point had flung the curtain back and now pointed at Muna's throat. She put out a slender henna-tipped hand and delicately pushed the sword away.

'I go to Meerut, to the house of a friend. I have no house here now, thanks to some fool who set the street of Harlots on fire. As to *who* I am – well, who art thou, that thou must ask such a question? *Everyone* knows Muna – if they be men.'

She had pitched her voice well; there was a laugh in the crowd behind, and a voice called, 'Oh Muna – do you leave us? What shall we do in the long summer nights?'

She looked past the rider, and leaned forward a little.

'Build me a house, friend – and I will return and make payment, in the long summer nights, the sweet summer nights.'

There was a roar of laughter then, and the rider half turned his head.

' Up,' said Muna to her carriers. ' Up, and off down the road.'

As they raised the palanquin, she waved to the crowd, crying:

' Farewell, friends – do not forget my house.'

The rider reined his horse back, and Muna, with a last wave, drew down her curtain and was carried down the road towards the river, and no one came after her.

She leaned back and closed her eyes. Danger had been very close. The rider was Hardyal himself. She heard behind her the sound of breaking glass and knew that the mob had opened the gate and was breaking into the Madoremahal.

' Let me out round the bend in the road,' she said. ' We must go across country to the river, and you cannot move swiftly carrying me.'

But the front carrier, Sakhi Mohammed, said, ' Nay – stay where you are, sister – if they send anyone after us, we must be seen to be on the road as far as the ford. Then they will believe your story. But if the palanquin vanishes from the road, they will start to search in earnest.' He was right. Muna leaned back with a sigh of relief which turned to a laugh.

' Sakhi Mohammed, never did I think to be called sister by such as thee ! '

The sowar laughed breathlessly. ' You are my sister indeed – anyone who serves the family is my sister. But my brotherly feelings could turn to something warmer at a touch – try me when we reach the hills, heart-breaker.'

They arrived, unchallenged, at the river bank, and waited for the ferry which was slowly crossing over, poled by two men.

' The Yuvraj and Rama,' said Sakhi.

' But what has happened to the ferrymen – and to our own boat? '

When they were on the ferry, and were in midstream, Kassim and Rama angled the boat into the current, and began to pole it down the river.

' The ferrymen were not there – gone looting, most likely. So we loosed the boat, the current should carry it down – and we will let this one drift once we have reached the old dâk bungalow landing place. How did you get on?'

Hearing Muna's story, Kassim frowned.

' We will have to leave at once – Muna, what will you do?'

' I will take her up on my horse, Lord. She cannot go back now. Hardyal would know, and have her caught and questioned.'

Kassim nodded.

' Of course. There is no thought of her going back. She comes with us. But she must dress as a hill woman – and Munabhen, wash that paint from your face – here, Sakhi Mohammed, give her my *roomal*.'

Muna took the handkerchief Sakhi gave her, and dipping it in the river, washed her face, scrubbing her mouth and her eyes. She lost years with the paint, and looked what she was, a beautiful young girl of sixteen. The hibiscus flower from her hair floated downstream before the boat, a little scarlet island. Sakhi leaned close to look into sparkling black eyes.

' She *is* a hill woman, Lord – see, the paint was but a disguise. Without it she is one of us. Where were you born, girl?'

' I regret to disappoint you – I was born not far from Cawnpore. But I have hill connections – Goki knows me well, and the Ruler – I was vowed to the goddess as a child.'

Sakhi Mohammed sighed and drew back. ' Such are the heathen – they sell their daughters into shame to bring gold into their families.'

Muna laughed at him. ' There is no shame in serving the goddess. All men honour me,' she said. ' I do not bow my head in shame, I am proud of my profession.'

Before her brilliant eyes Sakhi's stern expression softened, and he smiled.

' Yea. Each man has his own beliefs. I would be glad to find you smiling at me in paradise.'

For a moment their eyes held – then the smile in her eyes faded, and she made the sign against the evil eye, with a little shudder as if a cold wind had touched her.

' Look for paradise on earth first, and do not speak of your Muslim heaven – I would have no place there.'

She turned away, and looked at the sparkling water, and Sakhi Mohammed's eyes lingered on her down-bent head.

The banks of the river grew more heavily treed, and the current carried them quickly. Rama and Sita Ram poled in towards the bank, and nosed in a few furlongs up from the landing place. Sakhi Mohammed leapt ashore, and began to run quickly through the trees towards the old dâk bungalow and the steps that led down to the river. Presently they saw him stand waving, and they poled themselves down and unloaded the palanquin. The steps were green and slippery with moss, and they had trouble getting the palanquin up them. Once it was safely on land, Rama took the pole, and pushing the boat out, poled it into the centre of the river, turned its nose into the current, and diving overboard, swam back. The others were already walking up to the house, the palanquin carried with Muna seated in it. None of them allowed themselves to think of what they might find if things had gone wrong. But one of Sakhi Mohammed's men stepped out of the trees to meet them – all was well, and they hurried forward. Kassim told Muna to go in and find Goki and get a change of clothing.

There was another strange woman standing at the top of the steps waiting for them, a hill woman. Kassim stared as Bianca came towards him, her long hair swinging in a heavy plait, her white robes of *pushmina* flowing round her. Here, apparently unchanged, was the Bianca he had first seen, his uncle's beloved, her figure as slender, her hair as long and thick – but not as dark. The wide bands of white that striped through it, that was a change. And her face – ah, that beautiful face had changed. This was no longer the face of a very young girl. The sorrows and the knowledge of a mature woman, the lonely griefs of Bianca's life, showed in her face and in her shadowed eyes. Kassim took her hands and looked down at her.

' You are so beautiful, Bianca. You give me back the days of our happy youth – '

Under his gaze, Bianca's eyes filled with tears and she turned away from him speechless.

121

Goki broke the moment, coming out to join them, followed by Muna. The transformation of Muna was complete. Gone were the gold embroidered scarlet skirt, the little transparent gold tissue bodice, the gold starred gauze veil. Now she wore the same creamy *pushmina* robes that the better class hill women wore, and she looked young and innocent and beautiful, her eyes demurely cast down, her thick glossy hair plaited and hanging.

' So, Goki,' said Kassim.

' It seems we now have a collection of beauties to guard, as well as all our other trials. The men will go mad with frustration. Are none of our women ugly? '

' There is myself – old as time and wrinkled like a walnut,' said Goki.

' Ah, but what beauty hides behind that aged mask, what seduction sounds in that voice, shines from your ageless eyes – '

Goki cackled, and said, ' Well then, let us all be beauties. We be all of one blood, people of Lambagh, going home.'

Kassim nodded. ' True. Now, Muna, get you to the kitchen and pack what food we have – '

' No need. It is all done,' Bianca said. ' We are ready to leave when you wish.'

' Bianca – you are indeed a queen. How is Sara? '

' She sleeps again. She woke, seemed better, and drank some broth – but her fever is back. But she will do as well, carried to safety in the palanquin, as she will lying here in danger.'

They padded the inside of the palanquin with quilts and cushions. The food stores were brought out, packed into two separate *kiltas,* and then Sara was carried out by Kassim, and laid in the palanquin. She looked dreadfully frail and ill, in the bright daylight, and Kassim stood frowning as they arranged her as comfortably as they could, and covered her lightly. Bianca too was worried.

' That scar is a mark that will give us away if we are stopped.'

' Oh Allah kerim – I did not think of that.'

Kassim looked distracted. Goki bent over Sara, holding a small pot in her hand. While they watched, she smeared Sara's face from forehead to chin with a brilliant orange paste.

'To help break the fever. See, it hides the scar completely. It is tumeric and wood ash and atta – it will do no harm, and may in fact do good –'

Harm or good, thought Kassim, it does not matter – the scar must be disguised until we are in the mountains.

He looked round at his party, now all ready to leave, and it seemed to him that they would be recognised at once. Two high-born ladies, one of them wounded – an old serving woman who had spent her whole life with the Rulers of Lambagh, and he himself – his face was well known. There could be no doubt who they were. Muna was the only one who was changed – standing submissively beside Sakhi Mohammed, a bundle on her arm, she was just a girl, typical of those who lived in the hill States – and even she was a danger. What was she doing down here, so far from her home? He remembered then the Dhassera Festival – of course! They did sometimes come down from the hill States for the fairs and festivals in Madore City. He tried to put confidence into his voice.

'We will go in two bands – you all know the plans –'

'Wait, Kassim –'

Bianca was speaking.

'I have been thinking. If I go with you, if they find us, they will know us at once. Let me go alone, with Sikunder Khan and his son – I will go by Alnaghar and Shanpore, and down the hill route to Faridkote. They will not be looking for a woman travelling alone – and I can pass as a Punjabi Begum travelling to Amarnath to gain merit. It is a quick route.' Kassim knew she was right – except that the route she had chosen was the one most likely to be watched. He took her hand and found it cold and trembling. She knew as well as he did the dangers they all faced. For her, as for him, there was only one important thing – to get Sara safely back to her father in Lambagh. Reluctantly, he agreed to her plan, and her horse Bairam was led up. He lifted her into her saddle and watched her settle herself. Her face was colourless, but her voice was perfectly steady and she took up her reins in firm fingers.

'Kassim – guard yourself. May we all meet safely in Faridkote. There is one thing I must ask – how long does each group wait?'

Kassim said quietly, 'Only long enough to find Alan, and allow Sara to rest. No more than twenty-four hours – a day and a night. We should all be there within four days' fast riding from today – and I am allowing for our slower pace with the palanquin. If after twenty-four hours in Faridkote we have not met, then those who are there go on to Lambagh and tell the Ruler.'

She closed her eyes for a second, then smiled down at him.

'It is very well. Good-bye, my dear. My life is with Sara, in your hands – '

She wheeled her horse without another glance or a look at the palanquin and set off, followed by Sikunder Khan, his son pillion behind him. Kassim heard their horses settle into a steady canter, listened a moment until the sound faded and was gone, and then turned back to find Goki already mounted behind Rama, Muna perched behind Sakhi Mohammed and Sita Ram and another man with the poles of the palanquin on the carrying pads on their shoulders. There was nothing for him to do but give the order to start. This he did, so arranging things that Sakhi Mohammed led with Muna, followed by the palanquin with Rama and Goki riding slowly alongside. The other four men deployed about the party, and he himself was free to ride far ahead and then, having checked the route, to drop back and be sure they were not followed.

Chapter 17

Kassim watched his party start off, and himself rode slowly down the path to the river bank and looked upstream towards the city. He could see a column of smoke, but it was too far away to be the Madoremahal – probably the rioters were burning another street. Hardyal had obviously stirred the city into wholesale rioting – the fact that he had been at the Madoremahal with a following of Madore men as well as his own people was not good. Kassim stared at the column of smoke and wondered how many of Hardyal's men had been sent north to intercept Sara and Bianca – it was impossible that he had not done this. Hardyal was not a fool. As he sat on his fidgeting horse, danger seemed very close – round every bend in the long road ahead lay possible capture for Sara. His plans and plots to get her away suddenly seemed hopeless to him. He turned his horse and rode after his party, passing the old dâk bungalow, which now seemed a place of safety from which he had foolishly taken them all.

Although it was well into the afternoon before they left, the hours before darkness seemed endless to them as they travelled down the hot dusty road. Several times the palanquin was set down at the side of the road and Goki dismounted and bent over Sara – but the girl stayed sleeping, her eyes sunken in her face, with its garish orange mask. Goki folded her mouth over her worries. It would do no good to speak her anxieties, everyone was troubled enough as it was. If only Sara could have sipped a little of the sugared lime and water she carried. She did not like the deep sleep that now held Sara – it was not natural. Kassim watched the halting and starting again and fumed at the delay.

At last the sun went down and blessed darkness fell. He rode up and joined the others where they had pulled off the road and were sitting, their tired horses, heads buried in nosebags, beside them. Muna was gathering firewood, Goki was seated beside the palanquin, and as he came up he saw that Sakhi Mohammed had already started a small fire on which a pot was beginning to steam.

Kassim went straight to Goki.

' We have two hours – no more – how is she? '

' Kassim Khan – she has not stirred. I do not like her looks.'

' In the name of heaven, you cannot *see* how she looks with that stuff on her face. Get that paste off, and let me see her. Bring a brand from the fire.'

Sakhi Mohammed brought a flaring branch, and by its flickering light Kassim watched Goki clean Sara's face and then lay the small head back on the cushions. Sara did not stir. Her eyes closed, she lay, her face clean of the paste now, showing no colour but the purple flower of the scar.

' Oh my poor Sarajan – ' Kassim half whispered, and leaned into the palanquin, taking Sara close into his arms, straining her against him as if he would give her some of his strength and life. Goki and Sakhi Mohammed looked at each other and turned away, taking the torch with them and leaving the palanquin in the shadows. But Goki had heard the words that Kassim was saying, and her old eyes ran with tears. Kassim had forgotten everything, only the girl in his arms was real to him. Suddenly Goki heard him say ' Sara! ' his voice full of unbelief. ' Sara – '

' Bring that torch,' said Goki imperatively. By the light, she saw Sara's eyes open – she was looking at Kassim and he was bending over her again, but she pushed him aside.

' Now,' said Goki firmly. ' Now, my child, you will drink something.' Sara obediently opened her mouth and drank. She looked at the flaring torch, at Goki, and at Kassim, to whom she put out her hand and smiled. Then she turned her scarred cheek away from him, and fell instantly asleep.

'Oh thanks be to all the gods – she will do now. This is a good sleep. Now we can stop worrying.'

Kassim walked away and went over to busy himself with his horse. But Goki had seen his eyes, and wet cheeks, and nodded to Sakhi Mohammed who was carefully pouring out a glass of tea.

'If you take that to him now, he will eat you alive, Subedhar Sahib. Drink it yourself and then take his to him.'

'As you say, old one – as you say. Muna – bring your glass – or do you only drink wine and honey?'

'I drink tea with my brother – wine and honey are for other times,' said Muna sedately, and taking her glass went to sit beside Goki near the palanquin.

'She is better?' she questioned, her eyes on the tall figure by his horse on the other side of the clearing.

'She is better. She will gain strength every day now.'

'Thanks be to the gods. He will be better too, in that case. He loves her very much.' It was a statement, not a question, but Goki nodded, watching the girl's face. 'Yes, Muna. He will marry her – but not yet. He believes that the Ruler married Begum Bianca too young. He will not marry her until she is eighteen.'

'Three years and two months – he will wait. He is a wonderful lover. His love is like a great cloud that catches you up and carries you to paradise.'

Goki looked at her and nodded.

'I see. I see how it is with you. He visited you often?'

'Very often – this last year. I understand why now. But he is not as other men. He took me, myself, for his pleasure, knowing who I was – he did not close his eyes and pretend that I was someone else. When I saw that, I loved him – now I am caught and held for ever – but being without hope, I have only dreamed, and from dreams one wakens. He was never for me.' Her beautiful face was quite calm as she spoke, her voice quiet and reflective. Goki took her hand, spreading it out on her palm, and then covering it with her other hand, so that it lay sheltered in her old hands.

'I have wondered sometimes if you have ever regretted that I found you that day –'

Muna turned to her, her eyes brilliant in the firelight.

'Regret that you gave me life? Never! You are my father and my mother, my beloved old one – I have had life instead of death because of you. I regret nothing – only sometimes –' she paused, half smiling.

'What?'

'I am a woman. Sometimes I long for a man of my own, and a home and children. We all do, you know, even we of the sisterhood. But only sometimes. And never for him. He is only a dream. Nay then, old one, do you weep for me? I am very happy – truly. I have everything, including dreams. And do not forget – I also love *her,* that one in there. I will gain much happiness when I know she is safe and in his keeping. But I do not think he should wait too long. She is not a child. And she has hot blood in her.'

There was a movement in the palanquin, as if a bird stirred in its sleep. Goki leaned in, but Sara lay, breathing quietly, her scarred cheek turned away from the light. When she took her head out of the palanquin Muna had gone, and Kassim, having drunk his tea, was ordering them to start off again.

Sara woke when they raised the palanquin. This time they went across country, and they were all afraid that the rough movement would give Sara great pain. But she did not complain, only asked if she could have the curtain raised. This done, she lay, her scarred cheek on her hand, looking out at the night, until she fell asleep. Goki had put the pot of yellow ointment in her hand so that if they were stopped, she could apply it quickly.

By dawn they had reached Subhana, and skirted the village, going through the rukh that bordered the fields. Goki would have liked to buy fresh milk, but was forbidden to go near the village. Shortly afterwards Sakhi Mohammed dropped back and dismounted, tying his horse to a tree, well off the road. He was not long behind them – presently they heard him coming, and Muna, sitting behind him, was holding in one hand a full *lota* of fresh milk.

'The farmer will think his cow is running dry – but this should help to put strength into the Begum Sahiba.'

At the first stop, in a stand of dark mango trees, Sara was given some of the milk and drank it thirstily. Kassim did not join them. He was afraid for their safety so close to the grand trunk road, with the village only five miles behind them. Sara looked for him, and Muna, holding the milk for her, said quietly:

'He keeps guard,' and Sara finished her milk, turned her head and appeared to sleep.

This was a much used part of their route, and they saw men working in the fields, and drew off the road frequently to let bands of pilgrims, coming back from the hill shrines, go by, and traders heading south towards the cities and markets with their trains of loaded carts and ponies.

Kassim was glad when they took to the open country, working their way along the banks of the river, which was growing more and more narrow as they neared the hills.

That night they stopped in a ruined shrine under a pipul tree. The arches and walls of the shrine stood stark against the night sky, and someone had tumbled the small figure of the god from his place in the central niche. Muna, frowning, raised him and set him back, propping him in place with stones. Then she made obeisance, and turning away, began to gather firewood as usual.

Kassim wondered if the shrine with its ruined stonework and the faint smell of incense that clung about it would remind Sara of her imprisonment in the vaults, but she lay peacefully, her eyes looking not at the broken arches but at the stars above them. Presently the smell of woodsmoke covered all odour of old incense. Muna made an offering to the god of some flour and oil, Sakhi watching her ritual, graceful movements with a mixture of scorn and admiration on his face. Goki, whose sharp eyes were everywhere, bit her lips on a smile, and he turned away and threw more wood on the fire, sending showers of sparks up to the roofless arches, where they hung for a second or two, like fireflies.

Kassim, leaning on one elbow as he lay beside Sara's palanquin, saw her watching the scarf of sparks.

' You are better, Sara? '

' Yes – yes, I am – and I am hungry.'

' That is wonderful – here, old one – have we food suitable for the Begum Sara? '

Goki had nothing she considered suitable but milk – but Muna brought an earthenware pot of honey, still in the comb.

' Oh, Munabhen – how wonderful – you remember how I loved milk and honeycomb – do you remember our suppers in Lambagh? – '

' I remember everything.'

Sara put out her hand and touched Muna's saying, ' Oh, Muna – and so do I – everything.' Muna went back to the fire and Kassim looked in astonishment at Sara.

' How did you know that was Muna? '

' How could I not know? Did you think I could forget Munabhen, in ten short years? I have so often longed to see her – it took me a long time to understand that I would probably never see her again – and I did not altogether believe it – and I was right, for here she is.'

' Yes.'

Kassim's voice was odd, and Sara looked at him as if she would say something, but changed her mind, and said instead, ' I will never forget how much I owe to Munabhen. From the time when she gave herself to the temple in my place until now, she has served me in more ways than anyone will ever know. No one will ever keep me far from her again.' The soft voice held an unusual authority, and Kassim was astonished to hear it. Sara was not speaking as a child – she was silent for a little while then, before she said to him, ' Did you think I knew nothing about my escape?'

'I thought you were unconscious most of the time.'

'I was – but I remember a great deal. I have been lying all day, remembering things. I remember the wall, and Muna's voice calling me down – I remember waiting for you on the shore and Alan coming instead – I remember we shared a cup together when the Hakim was going to take the ball from my shoulder – you kissed the cup and said it was thus that lovers drank – and I remember last night.'

'Last night?' Kassim looked into the sunken eyes, clear and steady in the firelight. There was a question in them, and he leaned forward and took her hand.

'Sara, last night you heard me speak words I would not have spoken if I had known you could hear me. Put them out of your mind. The time is not yet.'

For a minute longer they looked at each other. Then Sara said slowly, 'Very well. But Kassim – is there a right time and a wrong time for words that come from the heart, and are not contrived? I do not think so. Do not wait too long to say those words to me again. Otherwise I might think you had forgotten them as well.'

Again this was no child speaking. The hand he held, tightened on his, and under its wordless command he raised it to his mouth, and held it there. Sara said nothing, but turned her hand in his grasp, so that his kiss was in her palm. Then she released her hand, and Kassim got up abruptly and went away.

Two hours passed, and the fire died down. Kassim woke Sakhi Mohammed and told him it was time to leave.

'Lord – is it necessary to leave now? The horses and men are very tired. If we leave at dawn, we will be in Gujerpore by midday, and we go by hidden paths now, all the way.'

Kassim looked at the exhausted figures all round him – surely it would be safe to sleep for a night? But a keener instinct told him to move on.

Sahki took his orders without demur. Sara woke and then slept again as they moved down the dark tree-grown paths.

Soon the shrine was far behind them, and dawn showed them the first outline of the first hills they must cross to reach Farid-kote and the gateway to safety. The air was growing colder, the river was speaking loudly, foaming between narrow, rocky banks.

Chapter 18

Twenty miles away, on a course parallel to that of Kassim's party, Alan and his companions had also stopped to spend the night at a shrine.

Their journey of two days had been uneventful. They had ridden by day, and slept by night, rising before dawn, and ending their journey an hour or two before sunset.

No one had spoken to them; indeed, they had seen no one, travelling by paths that did not appear to have been used for years, skirting one or two small villages, riding along the edges of maize fields, the corn so tall that it gave them complete cover.

Now, for a whole day they had ridden on the verge of a deserted dusty road, and had, as dusk fell, turned off and ridden deep into a jungle that spanned the road. They had ridden until they had come to a clearing, and found the shrine.

It was, in fact, only a plinth – the god or goddess who had been worshipped here had gone long since. All that was left was his pedestal, with an altar stone in front of it, an altar stone blackened by fires of a hundred or so years before.

' This is a very holy place,' said Rhada.

' They worshipped the goddess here once – until the jungle took over. Look how the creepers tangle in the trees. It will be good to get into the clear air again and see the hills.'

' Are you a hill woman? '

' Yes – I come from a valley near Lambagh. It is called Sindbagh. I left it as a child – I shall be happy to see it again.'

Walli Mohammed had lit a fire, and Ayub was settling a pot on it. Alan looked at his companion where she lay, propped on an elbow. The firelight threw a clear red glow on her face, erasing all expression. Perfect, chiselled, her head close wrapped in the cotton cloth could have been the head of a statue. He had seldom seen such flawless beauty. Her long tilted eyes were downcast, her lips curled in a small smile.

'You look like a goddess,' he said suddenly. 'Like one of the goddesses carved on a temple I saw once – it was covered with carvings, and all the goddesses had your face –' He stopped speaking, and felt his own face grow warm as he recalled some of the extraordinary things those goddesses had been doing. Not all of them had been looking quiet and contemplative.

She was watching him with laughter in her eyes. 'Yes – I know that temple at Jagganath. I can do everything you saw depicted there. We are very well taught.' She looked at him consideringly.

'I am at your service, Sahib, if you wish to experiment. We can go into the trees beyond the firelight. To make love is better than food or drink. If it would please you.'

Alan felt an extraordinary heat growing in his body, more fierce than any desire he could remember. He longed to take this woman, to lie with her among the dark trees, and taste all the strange wine of her loving, to slake this consuming fire in her body.

With strength he did not know he possessed he smiled at her and shook his head.

'I thank you, Rhada, you honour me. But –'

She lowered her eyes, and shrugged. 'Sahib – make no excuses. It was only to give you pleasure. I lust after no man – or very few. We of the sisterhood lose desire very early in our lives.' She fell silent, staring into the fire. Then she said thoughtfully, 'Sahib, you desired me very greatly. I understand men very well. I will tell you something. I know why you did not take me. Because you think you love the Begum Sahiba. You are wrong. You do not love her. You desired her – but her scar has killed your desire. You will suffer very much if you go on pretending to yourself. Forget your imagined love – be free, and wait for your own kind. The Begum's destiny lies far from yours. You should have taken me to ease your body.'

The combined shocks her speech gave him were like actual physical blows. He gasped, and stood up, furious, and was horrified to find that his anger was all the stronger because, somewhere, a voice deep within him said, 'What she says is true.'

Because of this voice he was cold and cutting in his reply. Rhada listened to him quietly, not looking at him, until he said at last, 'In any case, you know nothing about the English – and how much can you know of real love? Your kind of life, taking all comers for pay, a prostitute – how can you presume? – '

Under her steady gaze, he ran out of words. Then she said, unperturbed, 'You would be surprised at how much we know of both Englishmen and of love, Sahib. Did you not visit the House of the Lotus Flowers in Madore? I think you did. You speak very good Urdu. Did you not have a constant companion – one of us – oh safely clean, and kept in the *bibikhana* of your house – to teach you Urdu? Of course you did. As for love – well, it has many forms. We know of love, we of the sisterhood. Do not imagine that we be women of the bazaar brothels. We, from the street of the Harlots in Madore – you must learn that we are different. Ask any one of your older officers who have been long in this country. They will tell you. Ask the Yuvraj himself, he who is your friend.'

Alan's rage had died. He felt cold and ashamed, remembering how this woman had saved Sara and had helped to save him, and was now riding with him to help draw off pursuit from Sara. As he tried to apologise, she raised a slender hand to silence him.

'Oh, Sahib – never mind. Rage at truth-telling clouds the mind. Let us forget it, and sleep now. I want nothing to eat – I am so tired I only want to sleep – '

She turned away, rolled herself in a quilt and was instantly asleep, her face once more the still, peaceful face of a goddess.

Alan ate the hot food Ayub brought him, looking at her and thinking that indeed she was no common woman of the bazaar. He remembered the little frightened fourteen-year-old girl his bearer had brought him, virgin, and terrified of the Englishman. Well, at least she had not been frightened of him when she left him. They had learned together, it seemed to him. He had learned many ways to please women, as well as learning her language. She had no longer been afraid of men – she had been like a little animal, full of endearing habits, clean and faithful and passionate. When he left Lucknow, he had paid her well, and she had gone off happily enough with her money, having wept a little, for form's sake, he thought now. Rhada was as unlike that little girl as an orchid is unlike a daisy. Both are beautiful, but one is rare.

He fell asleep at last and dreamed he was holding Rhada, kissing her, and that she was turning to cold marble in his arms.

He woke with a start, to find a hand pressed on his mouth Kullunder Khan was kneeling beside him.

' Sahib – we have been followed. Take Bedami and go straight into the jungle, keeping the north star on your right – you will come to the road that we were making for – then turn again to the right and ride fast for the hills. I have taken the Yuvraj's coat and turban, it will serve you better to travel as an English-man going to meet friends at Ganjote. Wait there, in the dâk bungalow, and we will join you. If we do not come – then, Sahib, go to the police, and get an escort to Meerut and your own people. You will know best what to do then.'

All the time he was speaking, Kullunder Khan was packing what kit Alan had. Ayub led Bedami up, her nose bound with cloth, her bit and bridle off and a rope round her neck so that she could make no sound. Kullunder Khan tied Alan's kit to his saddle bow, and Alan, still dazed with sleep, the shadow of his dream clouding his brain, set off in the direction pointed out to him. Then clarity began to come to him and he stopped and said, ' But what will you do? Why do we not all go – ? '

' Because no one will pay any attention to us. We are three

136

horse traders going to a horse fair in the north – there are many of us about. We are quite safe unless they find us with you.'

' And Rhada? '

' Rhada will hide. She must stay. It is Hardyal who comes, and she can speak his language. We cannot. She will be our ear and try to discover his plans.'

Rhada's voice, cutting like a whiplash, a whisper as clear as a bird call, said behind Alan,

' Sahib. Go. Do not risk all our lives by standing and asking questions. Go ! '

Alan turned, and saw her, tearing off her clothes. As he looked the last garment fell away, and she snatched at a lota of water Ayub was holding and began to smear her perfect body with ash and water. Then Kullunder Khan said quietly, ' Sahib – of your charity – please go – '

Alan led his horse into the jungle, moving silently on the thick carpet of weeds and moss that covered the ground, threading his way through trees and creepers – more by instinct than because he was paying any attention to his route.

The truth he was facing was unpalatable. He was a useless member of the party, he could do nothing to help them, instead, his presence was a danger to them, as it had been, he now realised, to Sara. Kassim had seen this, and had sent him off as quickly as possible, for Sara's sake. To have had an Englishman in the same party as a girl with a scarred face – this would have been a stupidity.

Now there was nothing for him to do but wait. He looked at his saddle and found that he did not even have his rifle – that at least had been useful to them. The worst thing of all was that he was leaving four people, one of them a woman, in grave danger, in order that he could obey Kassim's orders and get to safety himself.

Alone in the dark, the darkness that falls in the last hours before dawn, Alan stood in the jungle, which is never silent, and listened. Was that a footfall off to the left – or was it a leaf falling from a tree? He untied Bedami's nose, feeling that at

137

least, if he showed signs of restiveness, he would have some warning if there was danger near him. He thought of several types of danger – tigers and leopards perhaps, as well as dangerous men. But Bedami was perfectly at ease, and he relaxed.

He had no intention of trying to find the road, and travelling on alone.

He was going back, to see what was happening, and take what part he could in any danger that was threatening the others.

He left Bedami free, so that she should have a chance of escape if she was attacked.

He was not thinking sensibly or clearly. He was wild with frustration and rage, and had an overwhelming urge to do something – anything – to prove that he was not just a thick-headed Englishman who must be kept out of harm's way.

Bedami lowered her head and he could hear her begin to graze.

His eyes were used to the dark now. Turning, he began to make his slow and silent way back to the clearing he had just left.

He had enough self-control to stop when he got to the edge of the clearing, and standing beside a great tree that was festooned with creepers which formed a natural curtain, he was able to see everything that was happening.

Hardyal was there. There was another man also, who was taking food out of a saddlebag, beside the fire, which had been made up so that it leapt and flared and lit the whole clearing.

Walli Mohammed was standing before Hardyal, while Ayub Khan and Kullunder Khan were half lying, half sitting, still rolled in their blankets like men roused suddenly from sleep.

Hardyal was questioning Walli Mohammed.

' Whence comest thou ? '

' From the Rann. We be horse traders.' Walli Mohammed was speaking Punjabi, which is different from Urdu, but which an Urdu speaker can understand. Hardyal was having difficulty though, for Walli Mohammed was speaking the patois of the village people, which is very thick. Hardyal made him repeat his answer slowly.

Then he said, ' From the Rann – then where dost thou go? '

' We go to the horse fair at Lalbundi.'

Hardyal looked across the clearing to the horses, Rhada's horse unsaddled and wearing a rope halter. Then he turned back to Walli Mohammed, ' Hast thou seen anyone on the way? '

Walli Mohammed stared at him in astonishment.

' But many, Lord – this is the time of the horse fairs – the roads are crowded.'

' Hast thou seen an Englishman and a girl – or a party containing an Englishman? '

Walli Mohammed's brow wrinkled and he looked over at Ayub Khan and Kullunder Khan.

' An Englishman – Lord, we saw many. They come at this time to buy horses. But we saw no English girls – there was this memsahib, a Colonel's lady, she who rides like a man, with a face of red fire – '

Hardyal cut him short.

' Not an English girl, fool – a girl of your race, a hill-girl – '

' Many, Lord. They come for the – '

' Oh may the gods aid me. Can you speak Urdu, fool? '

' I am speaking my own tongue, Lord. Urdu belongs to the towns. We be men of Kotlakhpat village in the Tehsil of Ferozepur – we be.'

Hardyal turned away. He gestured to his companion, and said something to him in what Alan judged must be either Tamil or Bengali, because he could not understand a word of it. Hardyal flung himself down beside the fire, and pulling out a silver flask, took a long drink from it. Then he began to eat, talking to his friend and paying no further attention to Walli Mohammed, who walked back and, rolling himself in his blanket, began to grumble quietly to his companions, a self-respecting man of the Punjab who had been insulted by a southerner.

Alan looked about the clearing to see where Rhada might have hidden herself, and then stood stiffly staring, his eyes refusing to believe what they saw.

The goddess had returned to her pedestal. Grey with age, with bird-droppings on her head and shoulders, timelessly beautiful, with downcast eyes and a small secret smile on the full lips, she stood there, as she must have stood centuries ago. The fire-light shone on her perfection, so that she was sometimes in shadow, sometimes in full rosy light.

Alan stood beside the tree, and looked at Rhada, standing on the plinth, a goddess returned, not two feet from where Hardyal reclined beside the fire.

A lifetime passed while the two men talked, not bothering to lower their voices. Then Hardyal yawned, and stretched, his hand six inches from Rhada's thigh. The other man repacked the saddlebag, and stood up, stamping his feet and pulling his clothes straight. Hardyal got up, and the two turned to leave. As they passed before the altar, Hardyal stopped, looking Rhada up and down, and said something that made the other man laugh. Hardyal put out his hand towards the beautiful body and then drew it back with an exclamation. Both men leaned closer to Rhada and then stepped back, and hurried away, Hardyal calling to the three men who still sat in their blankets.

' Watch your horses and yourselves. This is the goddess of the snakes – '

Five seconds and the two southerners were out of sight. Five seconds, and they were still within hearing. Then their horses could be heard stamping and jingling. Five minutes, and the steady beat of their departure faded down the road.

The four men ran for the altar but Rhada's voice stopped them. She still held her pose and her voice was a mere thread.

' Do not come any nearer. A krait has come from my feet to my arm. It is still moving up. Any noise or movement and I am dead.'

The flames of the fire danced and grew brighter as they licked round a piece of dry wood. A narrow brown shadow, small as a child's hair ribbon, moved on Rhada's arm – moved, stopped, and moved again. Rhada's eyes were no longer cast down, they looked out across the clearing, and far beyond it, to some other place and time.

The fire leaped up again, and the wood crackled, loud as a gun shot. Rhada caught her breath, the brown shadow was gone, and she said in her normal voice, 'It is over. Ayub, I have how long – twenty minutes? It is enough. Listen to me please –'

Ayub was already holding her in his arms, his mouth pressed to her throat, to the tender hollow where her throat joined the velvet flesh of her body. Walli Mohammed stamped with booted feet and ground his heel on a small shadow that wriggled and died. Ayub lifted his head and spat, and put his lips back to Rhada's throat, and all the time, she spoke, telling them everything she had heard, clearly and slowly. Her voice only faltered a little when Ayub took his knife and cut across in the wound, but she stopped speaking and gasped when Kullunder Khan applied the red hot point of the dagger to the wound. Alan could do nothing – Kullunder Khan saw the misery on his face, and said to him gently:

'Sahib – we are men trying to empty the sea with a ladle. Thou knowest, Sahib –' Alan knew. He bowed his head, and stood there watching.

Rhada had finished telling them of Hardyal's plans. Ayub, holding her close in his arms, asked for a blanket, and Rhada gave the ghost of a laugh. 'Am I cold in your arms, Ayub? It is the first time, if I am. But I think that I leave you now, and go with another lover, and he takes me into the cold and darkness. Ayub, hold me, it is very dark where I go – and I am afraid – I am afraid.'

Ayub's voice was steady. 'Go laughing, Princess of love. When did you ever fear the dark? See, the festival lights are lit for you, and there is music in paradise –'

The beautiful head fell back, and Ayub bent his head to her heart, and then stood up and carried his burden into the forest.

Kullunder Khan left Alan's side.

'I must go and help him dig. Sahib, will you saddle the horses? Bedami has returned – see, she stands there, with the others. We will not keep you long. The soil of the jungle is very soft.'

It was full morning when they set off again.

Walli Mohammed had gone ahead, travelling fast, attempting to intercept Kassim and his party before they entered Faridkote, where Hardyal had left his men waiting in ambush. Kassim, warned, would be able to by-pass Faridkote altogether.

Ayub and Kullunder Khan rode with Alan. They were men of his regiment, and he knew them well, yet now he felt completely apart from them. He rode in black despair, shattered by his own inadequacies. It seemed to him that since he had met the family in the Madoremahal, he had done nothing but bring them disaster.

Chapter 19

Close to Gujerpore, Kassim's party pulled off the road. Muna and Rama walked into the village and returned with food, and more fresh milk. Sara had the milk, and more honey, and then asked the question they had all been dreading.

'Where is my mother? I have expected each day that we would come up with her. Where has she gone?'

Her face was stark with anxiety.

Kassim, with Goki beside him, told her.

'She went separately. She has gone by Alnaghar and Shanpore. She took Sikunder Khan and his son with her and they were mounted on our fastest horses. They will meet us in Faridkote. Sarajan, it was the only way, the only safe way. You, your mother, and myself in one party – we would have been recognised at once.'

He expected her to weep, or worse, be furiously angry which would not be good for her. Instead, an expression of great relief relaxed her taut face.

'Thank God. I was afraid she might have stayed behind. Now everything is all right.'

Kassim thought of all the things that he feared, and that could still happen, but said nothing.

By evening there was nothing ahead of them but the long twisting haul of the mountain slope that led to the Pathana Pass. The river was far beneath, its voice a distant roar as it tumbled over rocks a thousand feet below. They rode slowly, the men carrying the palanquin changing frequently with the horsemen. At the top of the pass they stopped, the hill wind shrilling in their ears and tugging at their clothing, to look down into Faridkote, their final staging post and rendezvous before they began to climb into the mountains and through the high passes that guarded Lambagh Valley.

Sara was awake, and peered out, seeing the lights of Faridkote below, and beyond them, dim, barely seen, like cloud shapes, so high were they, the mountains. She drew a deep breath of the cold air and lay back.

Kassim was looking at those cloudy peaks too and thanking every god he could think of that they were within sight of safety at last.

Then, while he looked at the rampart of mountains, Sakhi Mohammed came to him.

' Lord. There is someone behind us – riding hard. I heard shale falling from the last bend but one behind us.'

' Whoever it is will kill his horse,' said Kassim automatically. Then : ' *One* man, you say? '

' I could only hear one horse – '

' That does not sound like an enemy. Take the party on, Sakhi, round the next corner, and wait for me.' Kassim looked down at Faridkote, so deceptively close, and shook his head. So *close* – and now, what disaster was coming, riding hard, pushing a horse into a fast heart-breaking canter up this steep climb?

He watched his party go out of sight, and pulled his horse off the road, and waited, sheltered by a great rock. It was growing dark in the valley, but up here, in the hills, there was a long dusk and the light still lingered. He saw, and recognised, one of his own horses, almost foundered, before he recognised the rider.

Walli Mohammed slid to the ground, and his poor beast stood, legs wide apart, head hanging, sides heaving to try to snatch breath. Automatically, as he told his story to Kassim, Walli Mohammed was working on his horse, loosening his girth, and unrolling a blanket to throw over him. Kassim listened to

144

his news and Walli Mohammed, seeing the shock and dismay on his face, said, ' But Lord, it is not so bad – you can avoid Farid-kote, now that I have been so fortunate in catching up with you. You go by Lungri instead, the path forks here, the old road will take you – '

Kassim realised that Walli Mohammed had no idea that Bianca was not with him. When he was told, Walli Mohammed, who had ridden like a mad man all day, could do nothing but shake his head and groan.

Kassim left him, sitting beside his exhausted horse, and hurried off to speak to Sakhi Mohammed.

' We cannot go into Faridkote. Hardyal is there, waiting for us. We will have to go by the old road, up to Lungri Pass. You will take the party on. I go to stop the Begum Bianca. If I ride fast, I should catch her at Shanpore.'

' And if they catch you both, they will use you as strong bargaining counters. No, Lord. You go on. I go find the Begum.'

Kassim opened his mouth to argue, but Muna jumped down from her pillion behind Sakhi Mohammed. She ignored Kassim completely.

' Goki – quickly. Is it possible for the Begum Sara to sit a horse for a short time? '

It was Sara herself who answered.

' Yes – of course, if I can ride in front of someone.'

' Good. Then we are saved. Forgive me, Lord – do you take the Begum in front of you. I will take her palanquin, and be carried on down into Faridkote, slowly, so that all can see me. I want to speak to Hardyal and find out where he is staying. They will do nothing to me – I was going to Meerut when they saw me last. I changed my mind, and decided to visit Faridkote first. All the north knows I am a hill woman. It will be easier for me to find the Begum Bianca and get her safely hidden than it would be for you. She will be in Faridkote long before you can stop her – and your duty is to get the Begum Sara to Lambagh.'

Kassim knew she was right. Muna nodded her approval of his good sense.

'I must have the same men as I had before – Sakhi Mohammed, Kullunder Khan and Sita Ram.'

Sara was helped from the palanquin by Goki and Sakhi Mohammed, who picked her up and lifted her into Kassim's arms. She wore a *poshteen*, a fur-lined leather coat that reached her ankles, and Goki had wrapped her head in a thick shawl. Kassim held her close against him, and saw that her forehead was damp with sweat and that she was terribly pale.

'Sara – are you sure you can bear this?'

'Of course I can – Munabhen, be careful.'

'I will – my life for yours, Sarajan.'

Muna, her hair loose about her shoulders, was carefully outlining her eyes with antimony, as she sat, leaning back in the palanquin. Her pose, her look, her very face and body seemed to have changed by magic. Here was no quiet village girl, this was Muna, the famous whore, the dancer of Madore.

Kassim set his horse in motion, turning to the fork of the road, the old road that wound down to the river, away from Faridkote, followed by what was left of his party. Walli Mohammed rode behind one of Kassim's men leaving his tired horse to follow unburdened.

The palanquin bearers, Kullunder Khan and Sita Ram, turned and set off down the road to Pathankote, with Sakhi Mohammed riding behind them. Muna rearranged her robes, pulled the curtains closed, and lay back, relaxed and at ease, completely sure of herself.

Sakhi Mohammed, that strong and violent soldier, who had fought and laughed his way through life, thought, as he looked at her just before the curtains closed, 'My love has fallen on strange ground – this girl, infidel whore, temple dancer or simple girl of the hill country – what was she?' She was not for him – and for her, everything in him ached and longed.

Muna's palanquin swayed through the narrow streets of Faridkote, heading for Arabserai the large Inn at the centre of the town.

Faridkote was a meeting place for all the roads from the north, and from the south. Here, in these streets, jostled Chinese and Tibetan, Afridi and Hindu, Sikh mercenaries and Punjabi Muslims – most of them traders, money lenders, or pilgrims on their way to the shrines in the high hills. Holy men of every caste and creed were in the passing crowds, soldiers going on leave, or, leave over, returning to their units. It was a town of shops and inns and brothels and money changers – and Muna, sitting in her palanquin thought, ' Even if I had not been warned I would know that there is something wrong here.' The shops and Chaikhanas and houses open, and well lit, still somehow gave the impression that bars were about to go up, that shutters would be closed. Something had upset the town, it was alert and restless.

Hardyal's men caught up with her as darkness fell, in a quiet street where the shops were already shuttered and barred. They called on her bearers to halt, and Muna's shrill questions were unheeded. Her curtains were not opened although men surrounded the palanquin. She heard a horse come up and guessed that Hardyal had arrived. As before, his sword raised her curtains, and, as a flaring torch was brought, he stared down into her mocking eyes. But this time it was different. Looking past him, she saw her men surrounded. Sita Ram and Kullunder were roughly handled and tied hand and foot. Sakhi Mohammed, pulled from his horse, was disarmed and held by two of Hardyal's men.

Muna swung her legs over the side of the palanquin and stood up.

' What means this? Are you Dacoits who tie up my carriers and hold a man of my household at sword point? The Panchayat shall hear of this and the Thakabar! How dare you molest honest travellers going about their own business? '

' I dare *very* easily. I meet you in strange places, woman who was going to Meerut.'

Muna, hand on curved hips, laughed at him.

' There is more than one way to Meerut. I met up with friends on the way – one thing led to another, and being a hill woman,

I then had a desire to see my hills again. Is there anything wrong in that? And who gives you the right to question me, Nawab Sahib? It is nothing to do with you, where I go.'

' It could be. I smell lies, woman. It is strange that we last met outside the Madoremahal – and now we meet at the gateway to the hills – perhaps a little persuasion with sword and fire will wring the truth out of your servants. You may find amusement in watching.'

Across the street, Sakhi Mohammed's eyes looked into Muna's. She turned away, casually.

' Persuasion with sword and fire will bring some form of truth, or untruth out of anyone, no doubt. As for amusement – if that is what amuses you, then by all means amuse yourself. I myself find amusement in other things. It seems strange to me that a man of your appearance finds his pleasure in such strange ways. Most men would think of other things in my company.'

She looked round the circle of Hardyal's followers, slowly, letting her eyes dwell on each man's face, her lips a little parted, one hand at her waist, the other resting lightly on her thigh. Her full pointed breasts were almost bare to the nipples where the bodice of her robe had been unbuttoned. The men shifted uncomfortably, their eyes on her. Hardyal stood there, and heard the indrawn hiss of someone's breath.

Muna shifted her position with a slow roll of her hips, and said clearly, ' But of course – you are different. You come from the south, and I have heard of your family. Boys, is it not? Ay me, what a waste – with those shoulders, and the hips of a leopard, lean and powerful – all to be wasted on a nose-picking boy. I shall be glad to find a man of my own race to pleasure me. I remember you well now. You are the man who burned the street of the Harlots, and left me without a house. Well, take your strange pleasures with my servants, if you will. But I shall remember you when I get to Meerut – or will you kill me too? For my men have nothing to tell you and will die. Have you such brave and faithful servants, Lord of the South who loves little boys? I think not – shall I prove it? '

She walked over and stood in front of one of the men holding Sakhi Mohammed, her very walk a seduction. Sakhi Mohammed did not look at her; his forehead growing damp, he kept his eyes firmly ahead. But the man holding his arm was already slackening his grip. 'Look at me, friend,' said the soft voice. 'Look and see what kings have paid for.' She stood not a foot from the man, then with a slow undulating step moved closer still, her eyes holding the guard's eyes. Sakhi Mohammed could smell her smell, strong and female, and his heart thudded. The man gripping his arm was shaking. Muna, with a sudden movement of her shoulders made her breasts jump and tremble, and her body came closer as she said very quietly, 'Touch, little man – let go of my servant and put your hands to better use –' The man's hand fell away from Sakhi's arm and he reached for Muna, but before he could grasp her she was out of his reach, laughing. Sakhi Mohammed stood where he was, while Hardyal uttered a sharp command and his guard was hauled off. Then Hardyal put his hand on Muna's arm. 'You do not have to hypnotise me –'

'Oho, Lord of the South – you would like to try the hills and valleys of my country? Good. We will make a night of it. But first – my servants will be freed – and there is the little matter of the price. I am not free, my price is high – even for a man like you. But possibly we could discuss this somewhere more suitable than the open street?'

Released, Kullunder Khan, Sita Ram and Sakhi Mohammed went with the others to the Arabserai. Hardyal had a room there, it seemed, and soon the men were sitting round the fire in the courtyard and heard, from behind the closed door, Muna's laughter, and then her voice singing love songs of the north. Sakhi Mohammed sat like a rock, his heart dying within him. His sword had been given back to him, there was no one watching him, nothing to stop him doing anything, if there had been anything to do.

Presently there was no more sound from behind the closed door. The men round the courtyard made up the fire and, rolled up in blankets, fell asleep one by one. There were two sentries at the entrance to the *serai*, but they were not taking their duties very seriously. As the night wore on, Sakhi Mohammed saw that they too were asleep. He moved over and sat with Kullunder and Sita Ram. Speaking quietly Kullunder said, ' What do we do? ' and Sakhi Mohammed said, ' We wait.'

Light as a whisper, moving like a spirit, in the last short hours before dawn he saw her slip out of Hardyal's room. She was beside them, and with no word said, the four of them moved over to one side and faded into the shadows of the covered colonnade that ran round the courtyard.

' We can go,' she said softly. ' He has paid, and will not expect me to be there when he wakes. You take the palanquin and go quickly and conceal it somewhere outside the town – if possible on the road to Lungri. I go to a house I know of, and then I will meet you at dawn at the Murree Gate. Sakhi, I shall need your horse, and I shall need you to come and wait, hidden, outside the walls for me. I must stop the Begum Bianca – no one else can do it, I know exactly the road she will take.'

Sakhi, his face haggard in the firelight, could not look at her and she saw his trouble with great compassion. She said nothing – there was nothing to say. One by one they slipped past the sentries, found the palanquin and set off, leaving her to turn and run lightly down the streets, turning to left and right through the narrow twisting ways of the town, until she came to a house with balconies jutting out over the street, balconies with heavily carved wooden screens. She tapped lightly, one single tap and four swift taps – the door opened at once, and she slipped inside.

Muna the harlot went in.

A Tibetan girl came out, young, rosy-cheeked, with purple robes, rich with embroidery, and plaited hair heavy with turquoises and silver and padded fur-lined boots on her little feet. She moved swiftly and was outside the Murree Gate before dawn. All around her people were stirring, the morning fires were being lit, traders leaving that day were readying their horses, loading their goods. No one looked at her. She found Sakhi

Mohammed and his horse and mounted easily, gathering the reins and saying to him quietly, ' Wait for me. Go in to the town now, to the house on the corner of the blacksmith's street, with the carved wooden lattices. Tell them that I sent you, and wait three days. Then, if I do not come, go to Lambagh and tell them where you last saw me, and where Hardyal was.'

She went then, with no farewell, and no backward look – and Sakhi, his heart rebellious but still ruled by his mind, did as she said and gained the house, and shelter, undisturbed.

Chapter 20

Bianca had ridden the well-remembered roads without trouble. Sikunder and his son made camp each night, choosing places where there were others, building their fire, cooking food, and bringing it to her. She had eaten, slept, and risen, lost in dreams of the past. Her father and mother travelled with her, and at each camping site she remembered those other camps, when her father had usually found old friends waiting, to talk over old battles – and her mother had been welcomed, with her daughter, into little whitewashed mud-bricked houses, and laughter and the sound of zither and singing had continued late into the nights.

The boy, riding pillion behind his father, thought she looked like a queen from one of the old tales, a queen enchanted into silence by a demon king. Sikunder did not think anything. He wanted, with every fibre of his being, to win safely through to Faridkote, make the rendezvous, and then reach Lambagh, with his son safely in his mother's arms, and his mistress handed into the Ruler's keeping. He could remember her as the beautiful child who had been brought to Lambagh by the young Sher Khan before he became Ruler, and he remembered the marriage. The reason for the ten years that she had spent away in Madore he did not understand, but now she was returning, and he did not desire anything to go wrong with the return.

One stage away from Faridkote they were sitting round their fire at dusk, a little distance from many other groups of travellers, when a newcomer cantered up, a girl on a big bay horse. People stared, for girls did not travel the roads alone. Then, seeing the thick purple robes, the tight, many plaited hair-style and the short curved sword at her waist they looked away. Tibetan women were as free as their men, and so close to the hill country there were many of them on the roads.

Sikunder looked once at the horse, and spoke low to Bianca.

' Sahiba – that girl rides Sakhi Mohammed's horse – see, there, between our fire and the Dacca merchant's camp – '

' I see,' said Bianca. ' Sikunder, that girl, the Tibetan – '

' That is no Tibetan. That is Muna. Wait, Sahiba.'

So they waited, and watched.

Muna chose a place, and dismounted, looking to her horse's comfort, and then started to make a fire. Closer and closer she came gathering firewood, until she was in shadow and near enough to speak.

' The tenth mile towards Faridkote, at four hours before dawn.'

She had moved on before Sikunder had got the sense of what she said. But both the boy and Bianca had heard.

In the small cold hours they saddled up, seeing that the girl had already gone. No one was disturbed by their going. The roads in the north were safe now that the British Raj held the country so firmly. Travellers in the north moved whenever it suited them.

They hurried down the dark road, and presently saw a figure waiting under the trees, heard the sound of ringing bridle and bit as the tethered horse tossed his head. Muna stepped out to meet them, and said, ' Let us ride on, Sahiba, and talk as we ride.'

Four miles from Faridkote they turned aside, and pulled into a grove of trees, and there dismounted, and sat – Muna and Bianca close together, Sikunder guarding the horses, and the bright-eyed boy watching the road as the first streaks of dawn light began to widen in the sky.

Bianca had listened to all that Muna had said about Hardyal

lying in wait for her in Faridkote. Her relief was greatest when she heard that Sara and Kassim had got safely away, and that Alan would also take the other route to Lambagh. 'You will probably catch up with them at the Lungri Pass – your horses are fresh and fast,' Muna had said. It was then that Bianca had asked if they could stop for a short time to talk.

Once they were settled, Bianca turned to Muna.

' So it is only me that he can capture now.'

' If the gods have been kind, yes – but if he captures you, he will use you as a hostage to bargain with – '

' I wonder if he realises that possibly my value is not very high – '

' Sahiba – you know the Ruler would do anything to get you out of Hardyal's clutches, and back to Lambagh.'

' After ten years? I wonder. Listen, Muna, I have a plan, and I want you to tell me if my plan is a possible one or not.'

Muna listened to the husky, hurrying words, and then sat thinking. The look she gave Bianca when she finally spoke, had both surprise and admiration in it.

' It is a great risk for you, Sahiba – but it is possible. I could have done something like this – but I see, that for your sake, it must be you. It is a hard way to win freedom.'

'Yes. But I win freedom from fear for so many people – and for myself? What do I win? I think I would gain a healing that I can gain no other way. Now, Muna, tell me what you think of my plan.'

Sikunder watched the two women with suspicion. He did not like being shut out like this, they were obviously planning something – and if anything happened to the Begum of Lambagh, he would be held responsible. Already the sun was up and the road busy with travellers. Surely it was foolish to continue to linger so close to Faridkote if Hardyal was near. Finally he voiced his unease and his Begum told him to be at peace.

' Hardyal waits to take me quietly in Faridkote, hoping to catch the others with me. He knows we are meeting there, and will not stir from the town for fear of missing us. Now, Muna, we will wait here until you bring me all I shall need.'

'I think you go right into the centre of the grove. You will be safe there – this is one of the places where there was a shrine to Kali, and no one ventures far into Kali's woods. Sikunder, make only a small cooking fire – and keep good watch. I will be here by sunset tomorrow.'

So, for twenty-four hours the three travellers stayed, deep in the dark close-growing mango grove where no patch of sun bigger than a man's hand reached them. They sat in the green and black shadows, and while the boy kept watch, Sikunder looked after the horses, who did not care for the grove but were uneasy, their skin twitching, though in that deep shadow there did not seem to be any flies.

Bianca sat, deep in thought, still as a stone woman, her hands folded in her lap. The trees moved and sighed, in a wind that had lost strength by the time it had penetrated the thicket where they sat. A bird, unseen, shrieked, and shrieked again, but Bianca did not even raise her eyes. Sikunder, his nerves strung tight by all the silence and shadow jumped, as he thought furiously, like an hysterical girl – but the Begum, her beautiful eyes fixed on nothing, did not notice. When she finally spoke, it was to ask how much water they had. The boy, who had explored a little, said there was a tank of clear water quite close, near a small ruined shrine. The Begum got up at once and followed the boy, and did not come back for an hour. Questioned, the boy said she was bathing, and washing her hair.

Bianca, standing naked on the steps of the small tank found the water clear and cold. There must have been a spring. The shrine was broken, and the goddess, dancing, had been hacked and broken too – yet still retained a kind of strange perfection. There was a great banyan tree growing beside the shrine; its roots spreading unchecked were pushing aside the stone blocks before the altar. Bianca bathed and washed her hair quickly, not turning her back on the shrine. She felt as if another woman was there, watching her. Finally, wringing the water out of her hair, she went to stand before the little figure. It was as if

155

someone waited for her to speak. She said, her voice sounding loud, ' Give me strength and success in what I must do – it is a fit sacrifice – ' and within her head, unheard by her ears, but clearer than the spoken word, a voice replied, ' Go, sister – and make the sacrifice in my name. You will succeed. A goat for Kali. I grow thirsty these days.' Bianca stood another minute, caught by a force so powerful that she lost her breath and almost fainted. Then, as quickly as she had been caught, she was freed again, and could turn and hurry back to Sikunder and the horses, her wet hair down about her shoulders.

Muna came before sunset, with a very ornamented palanquin, carved and inlaid with different coloured woods, and two strangers to carry it. Bianca went further into the wood and changed her clothes, putting on the beautiful cream-coloured robe that Muna had brought, a robe that fell to her feet, with small buttons from high embroidered collar to hem. Her hair was left loose on her shoulders, and covered by a gauze veil so fine that it lifted and floated with every movement. Bianca stood before Muna with the last of the sunset making a fiery glow beyond the dark trees.

' I will do ? '

' You will do. My heart and soul are with you. You remember how to find the House of Paradise? Because there will be no one to guide you – afterwards.'

' I remember. You will know if I am unsuccessful – '

' I will know. It is the top button, Sahiba. Do not forget it.'

Sikunder, called, received his orders in blank amazement. He was to go, with his son, and the horses, to the Lungri Pass at once – leaving the Begum Sahiba alone with two strange carrying coolies and no one else.

' I regret – but I cannot accept that order, Begum Sahiba.'

Muna sighed, and a powerful figure stepped from the trees. Before Sikunder had seen what was happeninng, he was felled by a blow, caught before he touched the ground, and put across the saddle of Sakhi Mohammed's horse.

The boy, seeing his father knocked unconscious by his father's oldest friend, was confused to tears and comforted by being held warmly in the scented embrace of the Begum. ' Your father was too loyal and would not leave me. He will wake with a sore head, on the way to Lungri Pass – we have not time to explain to him. Now, you go with him and tell him when he wakes that all is well – '

Muna mounted her horse and made off, Sakhi Mohammed, with Sikunder still peacefully oblivious and the big-eyed boy with a horse to himself, went away, and Bianca stepped into the elaborate cushioned and curtained palanquin and was lifted and carried at a fast trot into Faridkote.

They were at the gates of the Arabserai when she knew that they were surrounded. The palanquin was put down suddenly, and she heard running feet and knew that the coolies, true to the type they were supposed to represent, had bolted.

Alone, she waited, hearing men all around her. When the curtains were opened she knew who would open them.

It had been a long time, but as if a serpent had touched her she felt her flesh tighten and crawl, looking up at the man who stood smiling at her. Torchlight showed her that she was in a walled courtyard, opening off the *serai* itself – obviously a part reserved for important travellers who paid. For a moment she felt a dreadful fear – what madness had come upon her that she had allowed herself to fall into this man's hands? Then deep within her a voice said, ' A goat for Kali – ' and she was mistress of herself again.

Hardyal held out his hand.

' Welcome, Begum Sahiba. It has been many years – and each year has added to your beauty. Come – let us renew our acquaintance – ' Ignoring his hand, she stepped out of the palanquin and stood looking about her.

' Your servants chose a sensible part and ran away. You are ill served, Begum Sahiba. I will take better care of you. Please – let us not stand here – enter – '

' Since I have no choice,' said Bianca and walked in.

Inside the ordinary *serai* room were carpets and silk cushions and silver lamps and furnishings that would have been at home in a palace.

'You make yourself very comfortable, Nawab Sahib' – Bianca sank down and lay back against rose silk cushions, beside a low table holding a great alabaster bowl of white roses.

'So you do remember me – I have never forgotten you. How could I, after that unforgettable night we shared? – '

Again, like a bell ringing far back in her mind the voice sounded – 'A goat for Kali.'

He was wearing cream brocade, cut to fit his splendid figure like a glove. An enormous ruby hung on a chain round his neck. Bare-headed, magnificent, he was very conscious of his own looks, preening himself, one hand resting lightly on a dagger at his hip, a male animal of splendour, his sleepy heavy-lidded eyes raking her body as she reclined before him.

'Of course I recognise you. As you say, how could I forget? I have been expecting to be either killed or captured at any time during the last ten days.'

'Ten days? But when did you leave Madore? '

'Oh – nearly two weeks ago,' lied Bianca. 'As soon as I knew Sara was in safety – '

'Sara, where is she? '

'Nawab Sahib, do you expect me to tell you? Do not be foolish.'

He forgot to be charming. 'There are ways to make you talk – '

'No doubt. I feel sure you know them *all*. You know so much. I can remember – ' She lowered her lashes over her eyes, as one who thinks of other days.

'What do you remember? '

'Oh this and that. Why have you brought me here, Nawab Sahib? I am no use to you. In fact, even if you force me to tell you where Sara is, there is nothing you can do – she has escaped you, Hardyal.'

'But I have you to bargain with – '

'I am of no bargaining value, I am afraid. As you must know, I no longer live in Lambagh. No one is going to pay any ransom for me.'

' I do not need a ransom. Do I look like a pauper?'

' Indeed, no – such luxury! So – why am I here?'

' Because the Ruler will give me what I want, to get you back.'

' What do you want?'

' Among other things – Sara.'

There were white roses beside her. Across the room a silver bowl held roses of such a dark red that they were almost purple. Bianca saw the brand on Sara's cheek as she looked at them. Again the voice tolled far away, ' A goat for Kali.'

' I fear you will be disappointed, Nawab Sahib. A discarded wife is not a good bargain for a daughter who is also an heir. You have wasted your time, alas.'

' Then I will find another reason.'

' Now, what could that be? – '

' I could send Sher Khan one of your hands – and promise him the other if he does not do as I wish – '

' One of my hands?' Bianca held up her right hand, turning it this way and that as she examined it.

' I do not think he would be interested, really.'

' We could try – '

' Yes, so you could. Think of the embarrassment if he returned it.'

' You are very unafraid, Begum Sahiba.'

Bianca shrugged. The movement stirred the soft material of her robe and Hardyal moved suddenly.

' We waste time. Let us at least think of other pleasant reasons – while we wait.'

' Pleasant reasons for holding me here? What could they be?'

' Your mirror could perhaps tell you.'

' But I had thought – or heard? – that your interests are really elsewhere – and that you have to be drugged to enjoy women.'

' That is not true. No. *My* interests are – well, shall I say, all-embracing? – '

He stood, splendidly good to look at, his arms spread wide, smiling.

He is, thought Bianca studying him, very handsome. A most beautiful animal – and a very vain man, rotten at the heart; like a crocodile, he will stink as soon as he is dead. 'A goat for Kali' whispered the voice at the core of her being. 'A goat –' She watched the ruby glowing on his chest and noted how the burning spark at its heart seemed to flash more quickly now.

'When you say "all-embracing", does that include, by any chance, goats and camels? I had heard,' said Bianca delicately, 'I *had* heard that in the south, among people of your religion –'

He dropped his arms, and his mouth looked less generous. 'Goats and camels are an exclusively Muslim interest. We of the south – *we* enjoy the flowers of love – not the dung that grows them.'

'Charmingly put – how very charming,' said his companion. She had picked up a rose, and was holding it across her lips with one hand. The other hand was playing with the buttons at her throat. Hardyal watched that slender hand with interest.

'You are more beautiful now, I think, because you are older –'

'Now, that is a delightful thing to say – you surely have a gift for charming women. Is that why you drug them into submission?'

'You torment me –' said Hardyal, stormily.

'I? I am in no position to torment anyone. Dragged from my palanquin, imprisoned against my will, thirsty and starved, and, I suspect, in imminent danger of rape – and *I* torment *you*. Really, Nawab Sahib.'

'I *do not rape*,' said Hardyal. He clapped his hands and glared at her. When the servant came, Hardyal shouted at him and the man backed out hurriedly, returning with two silver goblets filled to the brim with wine as red as Hardyal's ruby, and small cakes covered with almonds.

'Drugged?' asked Bianca with interest, taking her wine.

'No!' said Hardyal. He had raised his voice, and she her eyebrows at his tone. He subsided sulkily, and she held out her glass.

' In that case you will forgive me if I ask you to change goblets – remembering what happened last time? '

He took her glass immediately.

' Ah – so it *is* all right – *what* a relief.' Bianca drank deeply, watching Hardyal do the same.

She lay back, her long silver-streaked hair lying all about her, and sipped her wine, her free hand holding the rose.

Hardyal, watching her across his glass said suddenly, ' Yes. More beautiful. Perfect. But unafraid, in spite of the cargo of sweetness you carry – and not wishing to be drugged. Strange. You are very unafraid – why? '

She saw sudden suspicion growing in his face and smiled full into his eyes.

' Perhaps because of clouded memories – drugs are not always good.'

' Clouded memories – what do you mean? '

She had put down her rose, and was methodically undoing the long line of buttons down, and down; his eyes, fascinated, watched the long white fingers as they moved.

' I mean this,' she said, her eyes watching him, as he watched her. ' I mean that perhaps, this time, I wish to know fully what I am doing – and what is being done – '

The last button was undone, the robe slipped off.

' Is that man likely to return? ' asked Bianca, white and silver and rose, smiling among the cushions.

Hardyal got up, stumbled to the door, shouted an order and locked the door, and came back to look down at her, lying pliant and welcoming at his feet.

' No one will disturb us,' said Hardyal.

' Then – let us drink to our present enjoyment.' She raised her goblet in a steady hand and drained it, and threw the goblet away, so that it rang like a bell on the stone floor. ' A goat for Kali,' said the bell.

Hardyal drank deeply, but did not finish his goblet. Mad with impatience, he fell to his knees beside her and buried his face and his groping hands in the white and rose of her body.

Ten minutes later Bianca struggled free and looked down at the contorted figure on the floor. It seemed to her that another woman stood beside her and looked down, and a deeply satisfied sigh sounded in her ears.

She felt cold, and drew her robe up and put it on, her fingers fumbling at the buttons as they had not done before. Now there was no one else in the room with her – no one at all. But his drink was only half finished – had it been enough? She bent over him and felt for his heart.

Yes. Enough. She took the goblet and emptied it on to the carpet, where it left no stain on the dark pattern. Then, with repugnance, she pulled his body into some sort of order, and left him lying, his head on cushions, his contorted, purple face turned away from the door. At least she did not have to dress him. He had not had time to disrobe. She judged that his servants would be chary of disturbing him until he called, and were probably well used to him not calling for some hours at such times.

The privy door was easy to open. She muffled herself in the great dark cloak she had brought with her, and slipped like a shadow through the door, closing it behind her, leaving the luxurious room and its owner behind her for ever. She felt, even as she walked towards her rendezvous with Muna, a great clamorous freedom, a wild happiness, as a bird, caged too long, might feel as it flew singing into the free air.

Chapter 21

Kassim and his party could not move very fast. Once they lost sight of the lights of Faridkote, it was very dark, and they smelt and heard the river before they saw it gleaming, lighter than the night. Then they lit torches, for it was impossible to cross in the dark.

The bridge was a simple affair, two logs wide, and slippery with spray. The horses did not like it at all, and had to be coaxed and encouraged over. Sara was carried over by Kassim, and sat leaning against a great deodar tree while he went back for his horse. Goki walked sturdily over, while Rama guided his beast, slithering and rolling the whites of frightened eyes. Then the party were all across, and remounted, Rama lifting Sara into Kassim's arms. She lay against his chest, silent. It was too dark to see her face – the horses were picking their way slipping and sliding, the voice of the river was close and shouted so that it was impossible to speak. Kassim held Sara close and hoped that she was not suffering too much.

Dawn found them two hours away from Lungri Pass. It was a misty dawn, with drifts and clouds of mist obscuring everything. Here and there, floating in the clouds above them, were mountain peaks. A stretch of the road would open before them, clear to the next bend – they would see the barrier of rocks that was all that lay between them and a two-thousand-foot drop to the river below. Then the mist would close in again, and they moved slowly, keeping close against the high wall of the mountain slope, while the path beneath their horses' feet wound up and round and up again, slippery with pine needles and small rocks, with the voice of the river faint now, like an echo in the mist.

The sun rose, and the mist was opalescent, a glittering opaque shawl thrown all around them. Sara stirred in Kassim's arms.

' It was just like this when we left – when I was a child. Just like this. The mist closed on us, as we left the pass. It was as if a gate had shut between us, and Lambagh. We must be very near the pass now – the gate will open. Oh, Kassim, do you think my mother is safe – will Muna save us yet again? '

There was little he could say to her. He was so anxious himself. Sara, watching for the mist to part, voiced his thoughts, because they were her own.

' My father – ' she said. ' My father is going to be very angry with us for leaving her. Kassim, it is my fault. If I had not been obstinate, and had not wanted to show off to Alan how well I could ride, none of this would have happened. You see, you would not look at my riding, and treated me like a child – and he looked at me like a man looks at a woman. So I was flattered, and I did not hurry back once I had stopped Zuleika bolting. I took time to ride to the river with Alan, and to stay there, because he looked at me with desire in his eyes.'

Kassim's arm holding her was like an iron bar as his muscles tightened.

' You were falling in love – or imagined you were? '

' Never. Not for a moment. I had already learned to love for always. My heart was given for ever, and I cannot remember a time when I did not love you.'

' Sara, be quiet. You are a tired child. You do not understand what you are saying.'

' I understand very well what your heart is saying. It is like the thunder of the river in my ear. Your arm hurts me, Kassim, but it does not matter. I am not a child. I am a woman and I love you with my mind and with my body. When I see you, when you are near me, my whole body loosens with desire. Even now when I am wounded, I long to lie in your arms – I am like

164

someone who reads and learns the words of a song but has never heard the music. I can wait, if I must. But one thing I must know – my face is marked for ever. Is it repulsive to you? '

Kassim's voice was very shaken, as slowly, one by one she broke his controls.

' It is, I know, a scar, Sara. But on your face it is a flower.'

' Kassim, I am a tree laden with ripe fruit. Do not leave the fruit to dry.'

Kassim lost in a mist of his own, his blood thundering in his ears, bent his head to find her mouth and the sun burst upon them, laying the whole of Lambagh at their feet in a light so crystal clear that even the farthest peaks could be seen. They saw nothing but their own hearts, mouth searching mouth until the horse, unguided, stopped at the top of the pass and began to pull at the tough mountain grass at the side of the path. Then Sara turned her scarred face to his breast and rested, and Kassim took up the reins, and they rode down to where the village and the temple and the old palace waited for them, and their news.

Chapter 22

The trouble in Madore was known in Lambagh village a week after it began.

The Ruler, Sher Khan, had long kept a number of post riders stationed along the route from Madore to Faridkote, and from Faridkote to Lambagh. His plans were detailed and ready.

When the news came that the Madoremahal was deserted, but that there had been no signs of any of his family along the roads, Sher Khan began to put his plans into operation. He mustered a force of men, few in number, but mighty in war, the best fighters he had. He chose fast horses, good for rough climbing. He sent for the men he had been training in Governmen and Defence, and issued concise orders. Mumtaz Begum, his eldest sister and Kassim's mother, was present behind the throne, where a carved screen stood, at all his councils. For she would be Regent, until the safe arrival of Kassim.

' I know what I would do if I were Kassim – and I trained him in early youth. He will split his party into two or three groups, and send them different ways. Sara will be with him, I consider. But Bianca will travel with another group. So – I will go to Faridkote and meet with them there – and as Hardyal is bound to find his way there too, we can dispose of him for ever.'

Under his words and actions Mumtaz knew that his longing to see Bianca was driving him.

The weight of the emerald Peacock lay around her neck – she sent him off, in the early morning, with a smile that showed none of her misgivings. He went by the short secret paths that were unknown to most people – paths he had discovered and used frequently during the last lonely ten years.

Now Mumtaz looked up at her tall son and at the girl who lay in his arms with a great scar, purple and scarlet with inflammation, burning on her cheek, and could think of nothing to say. The girl had been a beautiful child only just out of babyhood when she had last seen her. Her son had been a youth. This was a man who looked down at her. It was going to be a difficult story to tell.

She said it all very easily, as soon as she had welcomed Sara, kissing her warmly and handing her over to the kind waiting arms of the woman standing beside her.

She said, ' Kassim Khan Behadur, bow your head.'

As Kassim, bemused, bent his head, she took the great emerald chain from her neck and put it round his. The gasp that his man behind him gave was an echo of Kassim's indrawn breath.

' The *Ruler* – where is he – what happened ? '

When he was told that Sher Khan had gone off with a small company of picked men to aid any of his family who might be in trouble, and in passing to put an end to Hardyal's life, Kassim, who had somehow lived through three weeks of strain and terrible anxiety, groaned and sat down at his mother's feet. That lady gave him a sharp nudge with her knee.

' Lord of the Hills – you are the Ruler until he returns. No one who wears the emerald Peacock can afford weakness of mind or body. You have your people to think of. Get up, Kassim Khan – there are many things to do.'

Kassim stood, the scar on his forehead throbbing, his whole body aching with tiredness. He disbanded his faithful companions, and asked that ten men be sent down to the Lungri Pass to wait for Alan and his companions. Then, followed by his mother, he went into the Chotamahal, so well remembered, so full of Bianca and Sher Khan in their happy youth. The Begum Mumtaz, watching his face, said, ' Now, my son, you eat. Then you sleep. The village headman and the guard commander will

167

come for orders this evening.'

Kassim interrupted. ' Where have they put Sara? '

' In the big room at the side.'

' Very well. I will have my food with her.' He walked to the arched, carved door, and knocking, went in. Mumtaz saw the eyes that turned to welcome him, and went away, pondering. A day must be chosen – an auspicious day. There was to be a wedding again in the Chotamahal.

*　　　*　　　*

Night in Faridkote was never quiet. Sher Khan, entering the town by way of a little-used hill road, and a water conduit, quickly told his men where to position themselves.

' Selim, you see that all are in their places and then come and report to me. I go to the House of Paradise, for if there is any news, they will have it. Come to me there.'

Sakhi Mohammed, unrecognisable since he had shaved off his fierce moustache, kept a ceaseless watch in and around the House of Paradise. He had followed Muna and seen her return safely. He had noted that not all Hardyal's men were in the *serai*. There were several of them that he recognised wandering through the noisy streets. Hardyal was keeping a good watch for Bianca's arrival.

From the steps of a *chaikhana,* he saw her palanquin carried through the gates, followed, well back, and saw it surrounded and borne off to Hardyal's quarters in the *serai*. Then he set off to keep his watch on the streets between the Arabserai and the House of Paradise.

There was one man he remembered well, for it seemed he was always with Hardyal. Haridass. He was the first person he saw when he came into the street that wound down from the *serai* to the narrow old street where the House was. Haridass was talking to another of Hardyal's servants. Close enough to hear, Sakhi Mohammed drew back into the shadows.

' So – the Peahen is in the net. Then the orders are that we go back to the Arabserai and take the others as they come. Go you and tell the men at the Murree Gate and from before the temple to leave and take up position in the courtyard of the Arabserai. I will find the others myself.'

He walked away, and Sakhi Mohammed followed him. Several times Haridass stopped and gave orders to men, and Sakhi was alarmed to see how many armed men Hardyal had in Faridkote.

Haridass was now in the narrow old street where the House of Paradise stood on a corner. But he walked on past the house without looking at it, and Sakhi Mohammed drifted after him. Silently, moving from shadow to shadow like a panther stalking his prey.

There was another man walking in the street, a tall hill man in duffle robes, roped close to his waist by several feet of dark oiled rope. There were many of these men about and Sakhi passed him without looking at him. But not so Haridass. He stopped in mid-stride after he had passed the hill man and turned to stare after him. Sakhi, well in the shadows thrown by the wall watched Haridass turn, and begin to follow the hill man. Sakhi let him pass, and followed, puzzled. The hill man walked straight through the gate of the House of Paradise and up to the door. Haridass checked and looked on, and then began to hurry towards the main street leading to the *serai*, and Sakhi kicked off his heelless slippers and began to run. He came up with his quarry exactly where he had hoped he would, just past the gate where the shadows were deep. The struggle was short and sharp, and as noiseless as Sakhi could make it. He put his arm round Haridass's neck, and clamped his hand over the man's mouth and stabbed him down twice, feeling the man slacken and fold in his grip. Haridass had pulled out his knife, but had not had time to use it. As he died and his hand fell loose, the knife scraped over Sakhi's arm, so keenly sharpened that even without pressure it drew blood.

The struggle had been quiet and quick, but Sher Khan, waiting for the door of the House of Paradise to be opened to him, heard it. Sakhi Mohammed, as Haridass slumped to the ground, found Sher Khan standing beside him, sword in hand. He stared into Sakhi's face, and recognised him. With an economy of words, they hoisted Haridass between them, into the garden of the house, and the door was opened to them and they went in with their burden. Muna was waiting with several armed men – the body was carried out, and Muna joined her hands beneath her bowed head and did obeisance to the Ruler. Divested of his duffle robes, he took her hands. ' Well, Munabhen – *is* it well with you? '

' Indeed, Lord of the Hills, it is very well.' Muna's eyes were anxious – Sher Khan was not the person that she had any desire to see at this stage of her plans.

But he noticed nothing. He turned to Sakhi Mohammed.

' Sakhi – I did not know you, without your magnificent moustache. I owe you my life – and the lives of all here, for that man had recognised me and was no doubt on his way to Hardyal with his news.'

' My life for yours, Lord of the Hills – ' Sakhi was still breathless from his fight.

He accepted a goblet of wine from Muna, and as he raised it, Muna said, ' But you are wounded – '

' A scratch. The last scratch of the dying hyena. He had a knife and it fell from his hand, point down, and scratched my arm.'

Sakhi found this a long sentence – he was still breathing hard. The scratch he made light of must have been worse than he thought, for his arm was stiff, and he found it difficult to raise his goblet to his mouth as he toasted the Ruler.

He swallowed his wine, and the world tilted away from him. Was this wine so strong?

Like a tree falls, slowly, Sakhi Mohammed fell at Sher Khan's feet. His sight blurred, and cleared again, and he found he was lying with his head in Muna's lap, and Sher Khan kneeling beside him, grasping his hand.

Ever since he had seen Muna seduce Hardyal, Sakhi Mohammed had been in great torment of mind and body.

Now all the sad and painful thoughts that had been oppressing him had left him. He felt light and buoyant and young again. The face looking down at him was the face of his woman, the girl he would love for ever.

' That wine is the wine of paradise indeed,' he said, and did not know that he was whispering.

' I had but one swallow, and am quite overthrown.' It seemed then that the night had come right into the room, the kind night that would let him be alone in the arms of his love. With the world fading round him, Sakhi Mohammed, brave soldier, great lover, smiled into the eyes that smiled so brightly back at him, and the last thing he felt was Muna's mouth on his.

' Enter into paradise, oh brave one – and may there be one there who looks like me to love and comfort you – ' Muna held her hands over the eyes, sightless now, that stared upwards, until they closed, and Sakhi lay like a man asleep with nothing on his face but peace.

Sher Khan picked up the knife, and she took it from him carefully, and wrapping it in a cloth, put it down beside the body.

' Poison? '

' Yes, poison. They know much about poisons in Sagpur. Hardyal has Hakims working for him and all they do is concoct these deathly brews, powders and potions. I met a man from Sagpurna once and he carried poison on him instead of a knife. He showed it to me. Just a pinch, he said – I took a little and kept it. Poison is a good thing for a woman to carry. Come, Lord of the Hills – let us leave him sleeping till his soul has learned the road it has to travel. Then the Mulla will come and we will bury him here in the garden.'

She took Sher Khan out and up a winding narrow stair to the big room to which the balconies belonged. There was a large bed in an alcove, spread with a red cover heavy with gold, and banked with cushions. In the lamplight it glowed and burned against the white walls, indeed the whole room was translucent with colour, like the heart of a fire when the flames have died.

Another room, obviously a bathing place, showed behind a half-open door.

' Muna – you were expecting me? ' Sher Khan eyed the beautiful room with its flowers and carpets and the wine jar and two goblets beside the bed with raised eyebrows.

' I was not sure – I was not sure *who* I was expecting,' said Muna quietly.

Sher Khan looked at the cream silk robe at the foot of the bed, an exotic gauzy garment with panels of pearl embroidery running over it like drops of water.

' This is not for a man – or at least, not for a man to wear. Munabhen – you look for the Begum Bianca? '

' Yea, Lord of the Hills.'

But – *here,* Muna? How would she know to come here? She would go to the *serai,* surely – there are women's quarters there, in fact a courtyard set aside for women travellers.'

' She was told of the House of Paradise. It is safer than the *serai –* '

Sher Khan came over and put his hands on her shoulders.

' Munabhen – you have saved our family already and ensured that our blood will continue, Allah permitting, on the throne of the Three States. I think you have risked your life again, but I do not yet know the story. Tell me, when does the Begum Bianca come? '

' She comes tonight, Lord.'

Sher Khan turned away from her abruptly, and looked blindly at the carved screens that covered the open windows. When he turned back, his face was controlled, but his eyes were very bright.

' And this room – is it prepared for her? '

' I had thought, Lord, you might be sent for if you had not come – '

' Her spirit is healed, Muna? '

' I think so, Lord – I think when she comes here tonight it will be as your wife, and with joy.'

She left him then to answer a tapping at the door, and he was glad not to have her bright eyes on his face.

But as time passed, he grew impatient. He went to the screened windows, but could see nothing. He held up the gossamer robe with its pearly raindrops and put it down again quickly. It seemed hours since Muna had left him. He would go out, find some of his men and go down the road to meet his Bianca. He opened the door and went downstairs.

Muna was talking to two coolies. They had left the Begum at the *serai,* running away as she told them when Hardyal's men surrounded them. No hand had been laid on the Begum – she had gone into Hardyal's quarters of her own will.

Sher Khan's hands on the man's throat were the only warning they had.

' What did you say – where is the Begum – woman, what have you done? ' Under Sher Khan's sinewy fingers, the coolie's eyes were popping from his head. Muna, with a sigh, rose and went towards Sher Khan.

' My life for yours, Lord of the Hills,' she said and made a slight gesture. The other coolie, his face grey with fright, raised his short axe and hit Sher Khan a sharp blow on the back of his head with the handle, and the Ruler dropped like a stone.

Under Muna's orders, he was carried back to the beautiful room he had just left, and laid on the bed.

' Bind him – and bind him well. If he is noisy, gag him. I must go and wait for the Begum. Oh men – what fools men are,' said Muna, closing the door on the toiling frightened men.

She sat beside Sakhi Mohammed's body. His face, shorn of its fierce moustache, and quiet in death, looked very young. He could never have been the man to fill her arms and still her empty longings, for he was a man of Lambagh, and would have kept her there, in sight and sound of all she wanted to forget. To stay too close to the source and spring of her hopeless dreams would be foolish. Kassim's face came before her eyes, and her heart ached. Where could she go, how could she escape this consuming love that was so hard to conquer?

Love was very cruel, a fire that could burn, instead of

173

warming. She looked down at the dead man who had loved her so greatly, and tears suddenly spilled from her eyes and fell on his calm face. She wept for all lovers, for the happy and fulfilled who must part when their span of life runs out, and for those, like herself, who loved with hopeless passion and would never find completion with the beloved. She was a dreamer who knew that dreams are not for ever, she envied no one, and soon her moment of weakness passed. Muna, who loved very deeply, could recognise true love in others. Sara and Kassim were a pair. They had a destiny together, in which she knew there was no room for her. She must make another life for herself, and she must go away from Lambagh.

There was the sound of light feet on the cobbles. Muna got up and went quickly to the door.

Chapter 23

It was very dark, and yet, as if her new happiness and freedom had given her a special type of sight, Bianca avoided all obstacles – there was a lounging figure with a rifle at the entrance to one street, there were two men staggering home late, from a drinking bout – she was in time always to slip behind a wall or into a doorway. Soon the carved balcony screens and the door in the scented garden were before her. She did not have to knock – Muna had the door open as she came up to it. Muna's hand drew her in, and on into a little back room under the curving stair.

'Well?'

'Very well. Oh very well. I am freed of him, Munabhen – he is dead, and the means of his going freed me for ever.'

She stopped speaking then, and Muna, looking at her glowing face and her smiling eyes, knew that she would hear no more. The top button of her robe was gone. All Muna said was, ' Come – there is hot water ready, and I will bathe you.'

As she poured dipper after dipper of warm water over Bianca, she thought how perfect was the face and the body before her – and now a happy spirit lived within the beautiful body again. Like a newly lit alabaster lamp, Bianca glowed with joy.

Bianca, as the warm water flowed over her head and body, was recalling another day – when Goki had so bathed her in the Madoremahal, and before the day was over, she had been fleeing for her life with Sher Khan, to a happiness so deep and complete that it had even blunted the memory of her mother and father, left to be murdered by the Mutineers in Madore. She thought of the girl – not the child she had been – and pitied her. Now she was a grown woman, and did not have to shut her mind to the pains and losses of life. She knew, with sweet certainty, as Muna wrapped her in towels, that she could live life, with all its troubles and disasters, and find peace and joy in it – and more, if only – The thought half formed, she put it away and began to towel her hair vigorously, while Muna dried her body.

There were clean robes ready for her. Muna dressed her, and then, with her little pots of antimony and lip colour and oil of sweet sandalwood spread round her, began to work on her face.

'Muna!' The husky voice was full of new laughter. 'You make me very beautiful for a long and lonely journey. Who is going to see all this splendid work? My horse? It will all be washed away by the time I get to Lambagh – you are preparing me like a bride for her groom.'

Muna did not pause in her skilful work.

'There is no reason why you should not look beautiful, is there?' She finished with Bianca's face, and started to comb out her hair.

'Am I not to eat or sleep before I leave?'

'As to eating, indeed you must eat. As to sleeping, well, it will be as you wish. I cannot coil your hair, it is too wet. Sahiba, come into the upper room – if you wish you may sleep there as long as you like – I will bring food for you shortly. There is a messenger –'

Bianca was on her feet. 'Munabhen – there is a message from Lambagh – and you kept me here primping and painting – where is the letter – upstairs?'

Her feet on the stairs were as light as the breeze from the window that stirred her robe about her as she hurried to the door, opened it and went in.

The man on the bed, bound, his grey eyes blazing above the gag in his mouth, stared at her as she stood, backed against the closed door, staring at him, one hand at her mouth.

Ten years since they had seen each other.

Ten years of nothing but short messages. Now, husband and wife confronted each other in furious and enforced silence on his part, complete confusion on hers.

It was the stifled raging growl that he managed to produce from behind the gag that startled her into movement.

' For God's *sake,* Sher Khan – '

She ran over in a billow of soft silks, and was tearing at his gag until it was free. Then, to an accompaniment of strangled oaths she started on the knots at his wrists.

' A knife – there is a knife at my belt – ' His voice was coming back. Bianca felt for and found the knife and cut his bonds. He sat rubbing his arms and legs, and she knelt on the floor, still stunned.

Then, as he got to his feet and started for the door, she cried out, ' Wait – Sher Khan – where are you going? '

' I am going to a reckoning with Muna, and her henchman – ' His voice was murderous.

' No – wait, Sher Khan, there must be a reason – '

Bianca was beginning to see what the reason could have been.

' There is no reason that can justify the assault I have suffered – '

' Oh wait – there is – ' He was almost at the door when she rushed at him and caught him round the waist.

He stopped instantly, his arms out from his sides, his whole body rigid as he held his breath. Then he said, speaking carefully, ' Bianca, I must ask you to take your arms away. For if you do not, I shall not be able to avoid taking you in my arms – '

In answer, her arms tightened, her head pressed against his back. Sher Khan parted her hands, turned and caught her into his arms locking his hands behind her, bending his mouth to hers, until their hearts, beating together, were shaking the whole universe and the stars were whirling off their courses.

The bed, disordered by his previous struggles, received them, the music of their love rose and soared and drowned them in an ocean of perfect sound, the fabled music of the spheres.

Chapter 24

Alan Reid arrived in Lambagh, exhausted and ill. His arm wound had become inflamed, and he spent his first four days being nursed by Goki through a raging fever. He did not see Sara for a week, but Kassim came every day, and it was the old friendly Kassim who came, not the sarcastic stranger who had told Alan lies to get him out of the way. Alan found it hard to reconcile the two sides of Kassim's character and decided that it must be because of his mixed blood. Now it appeared that his English blood was uppermost. He was obviously working very hard. The Ruler was down in Faridkote with Bianca.

'They are having a prolonged second honeymoon, it appears. Also a small war. Sher Khan had a cavalry sweep that lasted half the night. Then there were none of Hardyal's men left. The townspeople did not burn them with due ceremony. They threw them into a pit, threw earth on them and planted a mango seed in the soil – and left the land untilled around them. That will be a mango tree with very sweet fruit.'

'And Hardyal –'

'Hardyal is dead. There seems to be some mystery about his death. He was poisoned.'

'One of his own people?'

'God knows – but there is rejoicing everywhere.'

Kassim stretched widely. 'There is nothing but good news coming from Faridkote – but no one appears to wish to return to Lambagh. Ten years is a very long time to be apart from the woman you love. Meanwhile, get fit, Alan – we will have such a shooting trip as you cannot imagine.'

Sara came to see him, with Kassim's beautiful mother, the Begum Mumtaz. The long grey slanted eyes were obviously a feature of the family – Sara's scar had faded to a purple puckered star. He looked at her and heard Rhada's voice saying, ' You do not love the Begum Sara – her destiny lies far from yours – ' He looked at Sara and saw a scarred, small Indian girl, and wondering where all the enchantment had gone, felt cold and empty and sad.

When he was well enough, and went out to walk around and see the village, he found he was treated as a hero, the man who had saved the Begum Sara from worse than death. But this brought him no pleasure – his self-knowledge made him feel ashamed of his utter uselessness. He was sure that Sara would have been saved in any case, and he had not even fired in time to stop her being branded. Alan moved in a fog of self-pity and self-dislike, and the smiling welcoming people of Lambagh were very puzzled by him.

He had the pick of Kassim's horses, once he could ride – and rode alone, miles along the lake shore until he found a little white marble shrine and lotuses growing in pink-tipped beauty above their flat green leaves – the lotuses reminded him only of Rhada's slender hands, and the shrine, of her death, and he rode back in worse case than before.

That night he was asked to dine with the Begum Mumtaz – Kassim was there, and Sara, and looking at them, he saw their love for each other, and realised it had always been there. They said nothing special to each other, the conversation was general, but it was as if they moved inside an enclosed place, set about with fires of happiness that no one could enter. It was a splendid dinner, and splendidly served. Alan ate very little, and drank his wine as if it were water – and it had as little effect on him.

When the table was cleared, it was carried out, and from the dark garden a little gentle music floated into the room. A hand picked out a tune on a zither – a flute dropped liquid notes, soft as spring rain. A voice rose, singing plaintively and then a little hand drum took up the beat, soft, and as insistent as the beat of a heart when love quickens in the breast.

She drifted into the room on the tide of the music, moving as gently, her gauzes and silks lifting and blowing on some unfelt wind. She moved her arms and there was poetry. She wore something – bracelets? anklets? – that caused the noise of little bells to sound through the soft music wherever she moved. She stood, and with little graceful controlled curves and gestures of her body she drew for them the pleasures of love, the freedoms of the body, the joys and graces of seduction and surrender. Then, as gently as she had come, she went, as if blown on the breeze, back into the garden, and the plaintive singing arose again, quivered, poised on a high dying note, and was silent.

Alan was suddenly held in an enchantment of the senses that he had only once felt before – in the grove with Rhada. 'Who was that?' he asked, when he had been silent long enough to recover himself.

'That was Muna – wasn't she beautiful?'

'Who is Muna?'

'Muna is my sister and friend – you must know about Muna – Kassim Khan, you tell him.'

'She did not come to join us in the dâk bungalow until you had gone, Alan. Muna has a long strange history. Her father was a British soldier, killed in the 1857 troubles. Her mother was an Indian girl, murdered by the mutineers because she was living with an Englishman. Goki, on her way up here from Madore, found Muna beside her dying mother and brought her here. She was adopted by my uncle as his second daughter, but she gave herself to the Temple of Suranath to save Sara, who had been vowed to the temple at birth. Muna went willingly in her place – and was trained, and as you saw, she is a most accomplished singer and dancer. She has risked her life so many times in the last few weeks to save us – there is no repayment. She is known and beloved all over the three States, and we hope she will stay here now –'

Alan waited the shortest time that good manners would allow. He then took his leave, pleading fatigue, and left, grateful that Kassim did not either offer to ride back with him, or send an escort to see him safely home.

The garden was empty, the moon so bright and so high that the trees stood in pools of black shadow.

There were so many shadows. A shadow chased his horse, the road was striped with light and shade. When he arrived at the lake, it was a sheet of silver that shimmered and moved constantly as the night breeze stirred it. The moon cast a light that took all the colour out of the world, leaving it black and silver.

The girl, standing on the shore with her hair and her robes blowing about her, was as insubstantial as mist.

Alan rode over to her, his heart beating out the rhythm of a hand drum, his ears hearing the echoes of a high plaintive song.

Her eyes were large and dark and full of moonlight. Her mouth, in her moon-blanched face was like a dark rose. They turned together as if some message had passed, wordless, between them, and walked to Alan's house, each apart, not touching hand or arm.

His room was full of moonlight, spilling in through the side window. Her body, when the silks that wrapped it had been dropped, quietly sighing, to the floor, was like a silver cupful of a wine he had been longing to drink. His hands tangled in her long hair, he stooped to her mouth as a man in the desert stoops to a pool.

When she led him to the bed their love was a gentle thing, until caught fire from fire, and they were consumed utterly.

Chapter 25

When Alan woke, the room was grey with the first light of dawn, and Muna was lying beside him in splendid nakedness, propped on one elbow, watching him.

He put out a hand and cupped her face, and said, ' I love you – '

Muna shook her head, puckering her beautiful eyebrows.

' Love? What is love, Sahib? '

' Love is what I have for you – I do not know what love is, but whatever it is, I have it for you.'

' And when my body is old and dry? '

' I shall love the memory of you, and only see the memory. But you will never grow old – '

Muna, staring down at the palm of one hand, nodded.

' No. I do not think I will. But if you love me, can you tell me what I am? '

' I know who you are – you are Muna, the Ruler's adopted daughter.'

' I am Muna, the temple dancer, the whore – '

' You are Muna, the woman I love. Is that not enough? '

' I do not know. I am what I am, and cannot wipe away the past. What do you want with me, Sahib? '

' I want to live with you at my side for the rest of my life.'

Muna got up and collected her silks.

' Will you come back? '

' I will come back – with the moon, tonight.'

All that morning, Alan sat, looking at the lake and the mountains and the fish eagle hanging in the still, cloudless sky.

He saw nothing that was before his eyes. He was looking with the eyes of memory.

He saw narrow, winding lanes, with high hedges each side, tangled with dog-roses and ivy. He saw Kentish orchards and hopfields, and an old house, the bricks mellowed to pink, the long drawing-room and the candles reflecting on the dark dining-room table. His mother's face, his father standing on the terrace, sniffing the damp morning air like an old dog, the roses scattering scarlet petals on the bricked paths between green lawns, the clock over the stable gate – and he put Muna there. She sat in the drawing-room among the faded chintzes with his mother, she rode in the lanes with him, she walked the rose-strewn paths, leaning on his father's arm, she smiled through the candlelight, her wine glass toasting him – and she was happy.

He did not see, in his dreaming pleasure, the faces of his mother's friends, their eyes full of probing curiosity as they looked at his wife. He did not see the heads that turned in the village church, nor imagine the loneliness of a woman homesick for known and beloved ways of life, nor the miseries that could come to the children of a mixed marriage. He saw nothing but Muna's great eyes smiling into his.

He was lying on his bed, watching the moonlight creep over the floor when she came, moving like a shadow, her robes falling from her and her silver body bending to meet his outstretched arms.

Two tigers hunted the same jungle that night, and full fed, slept until the sun woke them.

' I love you,' said Alan.

' I still do not know what love is. I enjoy you – and you enjoy me. Is that love? '

' No.'

' Then what? '

' I do not know. Enjoyment is part of loving – '

As on the day before, she collected her clothes and he said,

' Will you come back ? '

' Yes.'

' The moon rises late. Come to me with the dark – '

' I will come.'

Muna waited outside the room where Kassim sat, listening to petitions, ordering the daily life of the three States. She sent in a request to speak to him.

He came out at once to take her in.

Muna wore splendid emerald silk, finer than air, floating and blowing about her with every move she made.

' I can talk to you alone ? '

' The room is empty, Munabhen – '

' Lord, I have a question to ask. Will you answer me truly ? '

' I will, Muna – ' Kassim was frowning.

' Do not frown, Lord. It is not a puzzle. You must know that I have loved you all my life. All men have been you. Will you tell me – could you take me, and keep me near you, and visit me from time to time ? Is there anything in your heart for me ? '

Kassim's voice was very gentle when he replied. ' You know how often I have enjoyed your body, Muna – but now, my mind and heart are full of Sara. I have nothing in my heart for you but friendship. You also know how long I have loved Sara. I meant to wait until she was fully grown, but she has taken time from me, I can wait very little longer, and cannot slake my thirst elsewhere.'

She bent her head above her splendid silks. ' Then I am free, Lord, and I will go from here. God give you blessing and great happiness, Lord, always. Do not forget Muna.'

' There is no one in the three States, and no one in my family who will ever forget you, Muna. Go with happiness.'

It was dark when Alan heard the whisper of silk dropped to the floor. As he opened his arms, she was there. They climbed among high peaked mountains, and were still awake when dawn came and threw purple and gold and scarlet on the peaks outside.

' I love you – '

' I do not know even yet, what love is. But I can learn.'

' It is cold and grey in England much of the time. You will have to wear a great many clothes – '

' Is this love ? '

' No – but the willingness to wear them is.'

' Then I am learning. Will I have a child ? '

' Several, I hope. Muna, we marry in Bombay before we sail. Soon – though I need a little time. I shall ask for special leave from my regiment, perhaps even a transfer. I think it better if we leave India.'

' Yes. I also need time. I need two months to arrange my affairs. You will lie alone till then. Where will you be in two months from now ? '

' I shall be on the station platform in Madore, on the 29th of June, taking the train to Bombay.'

' I shall be there. You will see me.'

*   *   *

Sher Khan and Bianca, living in a world where nothing existed but themselves, a world where each day that passed brought a memory, or a fresh discovery to fill them with happiness, still managed to think of Lambagh Valley, and know that they must return there soon.

Therefore, when a servant came to tell them that the dancer Muna was asking if she could speak with the Begum Sahiba, they thought it would be a message from Lambagh.

Bianca hurried down to the little room under the stairs where Muna waited, standing by the arched window, looking out at the quiet garden that surrounded the House of Paradise. There was something about the way the girl stood that momentarily frightened Bianca.

' Muna – is there bad news from Lambagh ? Is Sara well ? '

' There is no bad news, Sahiba – and the little Begum is very well, and very happy, and much in love with the Yuvraj.'

' Then – Muna, what is it ? You are weeping ! '

Not since she had once seen another friend weep, not since Khanzada had wept before her had Bianca been so frightened by tears.

' Munabhen – what is wrong – ? '

Muna made no effort to hide her tears, they ran down her face like rain, and Bianca looked at her and did not know what to do. Presently Muna wiped her cheeks with her hands, and said quietly,

' I do not know why I weep. I have no reason. Khanum, I come to ask your help. Listen, and I will tell you what I need from you. There is no one else I would ask. I go to a new life, and I can only do it with success if you will help me.'

Bianca sat with her, and listened to her story and her plans. When Muna had finished speaking, Bianca nodded at her.

' I owe you a debt that I can never repay – but this small thing I can do for you. I promise you that you will go to your new life without fear, and that you will be as skilled and able to deal with all that you will find as I can make you. Come, Munabhen, let us go and tell Sher Khan what we plan, and then we will get the best tailors we can find, and we will begin for you another training – which will be much easier than anything you have encountered in your life so far – because, do not forget, you have English blood in you. You will see how easy it will be. We have just short of two months, Come, Munabhen – we tell the Ruler first, and then we will begin.'

It was a strange period in Muna's life. She worked very hard at her new lessons. Soon she spoke and understood a remarkable amount of English. Bianca marvelled at her aptitude, for her accent was faultless. Muna learned how to sit at a table and handle knives and forks and spoons. She learned to curtsey, to bow, to manage the voluminous skirts and tight constricting bodices that English women wore, so uncomfortable after her own drifting silks and warm, light Cashmir robes.

At night she lay and wondered about her future. England was as far away as the silver moon that was full again, spilling cold light in through her windows. It seemed impossible that she would not see that moon reflecting back from the snows and the clear lake water of Lambagh. She thought of Sara, sleeping beside that lake, and of the wedding that would be celebrated there. Sara with her scarred face, and her warm loving heart, who would stay in known places, and live out her dreams.

Sometimes, in those nights of thought and sleepless watching, Muna would be afraid, and wonder how she came to be in Faridkote, learning a strange way of life, so that she could go away from everything she understood, from the country where she was a person to be respected and admired, where she was Muna, the famous. If things had been different – would she have been there in Lambagh, married and happy to know that life in the beautiful valley stretched ahead of her, one peaceful day after another? It was impossible to visualise. She looked back on her life without regret, and on Sara with love. Kassim she closed into a secret place in her heart, and drew strength from his presence there. She remembered the pleasure she found in Alan's arms, and began to think of her future with courage.

*   *   *

It was hot in Madore in June. The station was crowded as it always was. Alan stood outside his compartment, and the crowd surged past: white-veiled women with babies on their hips, shouting men laden with anonymous bundles, soldiers, both British and Indian, struggling with leave passes and unwieldy bedding rolls – Fakirs, Sikhs, sweet sellers, tea sellers and bewildered farmers encumbered by struggling goats and calves, and baskets of demented beady-eyed chickens.

In a sudden island of silence, just before the guard blew his whistle, she was there.

White-gloved hands held a fan and a parasol. The dress, of drifting grey and white muslin, was impeccable. The hat, perched on coiled dark hair, was veiled, a plain straw embellished with a single white rose. Beneath it, her face had the delicate creamy tint of ivory. Her dark, shadowed eyes looked gravely at him,

187

and she said, holding out her gloved hand, ' I am in time? '

Alan took the slender hand and kissed it. ' In perfect time. Have you a berth? '

' I have a compartment – my maid is in it, and my bearer is next door. But I thought – the moon is full tonight. I thought I would travel with you until the station before Bombay. That will be three nights. I can learn more about love in these nights, and perhaps more English.'

The Indian countryside slipped past, the moon lighting every fold of every hill, each little mud-walled village, each dark grove of trees.

Alan, his long waiting comforted, slept.

Muna lay, propped on her elbow, watching the shadow of the train running alongside over the fields and groves of the Indian plains. It was no use looking at the skyline, for the mountains were far away. The moonlight fell on her face and sparkled as if her cheeks were studded with diamonds. The train thundered and shuddered, and beat out words, like the drums she had danced to on festival nights.

Alan moved, and woke, and saw her.

' I love you – '

She lay down in his arms while the night, and India, rattled away.